Street Life Part 1
Freedom

Pepi

Cadmus Publishing
www.cadmuspublishing.com

TABLE OF CONTENTS

CHAPTER ONE

BLACK BOY LOST

James struggled to free himself from the five guards trying to restrain him. "Hold him down! Hold him down! Cynthia, give me the syringe, hurry up, hurry up, damn it!" When Dr. Weinstein pierced James in the buttocks with the syringe, he slid into an abyss of calmness, his muscles relaxed, though it felt good, James knew it wasn't good. The sedative they put in him, would have him sedated for the rest of the day. As he slid into a state of weariness, he slurred: "my name is my property, my name is my property." Hmmm, thought Officer Kaniski, he always says that, I wonder where he got that from. Officer Kaniski shrugged, shut the isolation cell door, and went to his post to wait the last three hours of his shift in the mental health unit at the Oak Park Heights, maximum-security prison.

James lay in the bare isolation cell, on a plastic mattress, with no sheets, wearing a yellow suicide gown. His body was relaxed and numb, even in this condition, his mind would not rest. He thought, I guess this is what it is to have freedom; or I could choose to be a slave, like everyone else. I won't worry about it, because one day, I'll expose the scheme to the world. Then his thoughts shifted to when he was in the world, he grinned, and thought, who'd ever think I'd end up like this. His mind drifted to Vino's house, where he use to be with his best friend Joe and the other brotha's. Those were the days, he thought; I didn't have a worry in the world, well, not that many. James met Joe in high school, during his sophomore year in a math class, which he hated and couldn't skip, because his father would kill him. So, he decided to stay and tough it out. Joe sat in the back of the class to James' right. Joe was a medium built Puerto Rican kid with long hair; he kept in a ponytail, with lots of energy, that's probably why they got along, because James was the opposite.

One afternoon, during lunch, James made his way to the local Burger King because the school lunch wasn't his forte. On the way to the Burger King, James past Joe, while exiting the back door, so he could use the short cut to Burger King. In passing Joe, Joe said, "what's up? Your not from around here; where you from?"

"My family moved here from Gary a few months ago."

"O.k., that's cool. Where you live?"

"I stay on 25th and Franklin."

"Snap! I live on 26th Street, you're right around the corner from me. Where you on your way to?"

"Up the street, to get a burger or something this school food ain't about nothin."

"I'm on my way up there too, let's kick it and I'll give you the low down on what's up around here."

As they crossed the field, and walked the two blocks to Burger King, Joe began telling James about the school. As they crossed the busy intersection of Lake Street, Joe began to tell James about the dos and don'ts of the school. "You gotta be careful when you see Steve, he's the hall police, he always sweatin people about being in the hall. And if you're late when he bell rings, he's takin you straight to the office; I can't stand that mark. All the shop classes are cool, because it's only half a day. I'd take advantage of that. You into sports?"

"A little, but that's not my thang."

"Whatchu into?"

"I mess with music."

"That's cool. What instrument you like playin?"

"The sax," he said, as he began to make motions, as if he were playing the saxophone.

"My pops use to play the congas in a band in New York, before we moved to Minnesota."

Looking puzzled, James said, "where you from?"

"New York by way of Peurtoooooooooo Riicoooo."

"How long you been in Minnesota?"

Opening the door to the restaurant. Joe said, "we been in America since I was eight, we moved to Minnesota with my aunt when I was thirteen, so that's about six or seven years."

May I take your order, asked the cashier? James ordered a whopper with cheese and a medium coke. Joe interrupted saying, "Yo Bruh, we don't eat no swine."

"What's swine?"

"What's swine," Joe said with a confused look on his face. He said excitedly, "pork. Your people eat swine?"

"Yeah, it's food ain't it?"

"Listen, if your going to eat with me, you gotta eat the right way."

"What's the right way?"

"The way Allah intended for us to eat; no swinin and dinin."

"Who is Allah?"

Joe looked surprised and said, "don't worry about it, dig this, he'll have a whopper with no pork, as Joe slid the food he ordered back to the cashier. While waiting on the order, James heard someone say, "What it do lord." He turned and it was three guys on the other side of the restaurant. Joe responded, "What up people." As they grabbed their orders off the counter, Joe said, "let's go over here." As they approached the three guys, Joe began to shake their hands, it wasn't a regular handshake, it was the same handshake James saw many times in Gary. James thought Joe was a vice lord. James remembered them at his school in Gary, but he never hung out with em, because his dad would've beat him to a pulp. His life consisted of bible study, church, and more bible study. Joe interrupted his thought, when he said, "this is James ya'll." The bald-headed guy said "where you from?"

"I just moved here from Gary."

"My name is Ray. He asked. Ya'll got some lords in Gary?"

"Yeah"

"Daaaaamn, the lords is everywhere. I told ya'll, this shit is universal. Anyway, this is Kev, that's his cousin Chris, we call him C. They sat there eating, talking, and joking about the neighborhood, girls, and school. Joe interrupted, and said, "We gotta get back to class." As they left, Joe shook hands with C, Ray, and Kev and headed to the exit so he wouldn't be late for class. On the way to school, James asked, "Aren't they going to class?"

"Them fools always skippin. I can't do it; I got in trouble the last time I got caught. I'm cool on that."

"What happened?"

"They had the police at my moms crib, and started talkin some shit, like reformatory school, and truancy officers, it was seriously mad. I ain't goin through that again." As they made their way across Lake Street and through the field back to school. Joe began telling James about the school, neighborhood, and how much he couldn't stand Steve's ass. On their way back to class, the passed Steve in the rotunda; James took note that Steve looked like he ate weights for food and stare like a lion. James thought, this is a big ass white dude, he look like a WWF wrestler, damn. No matter how much Joe hates him, He's going to have serious issues messin with that cat. As James took his seat, Miss Hawkins began writing on the board, and example about how someone paid thirty-two percent of their monthly salary for taxes, or something like that; James' mind began to drift to how he was going to do his after school chores, this dumb ass math homework, oh an how his dad was doing bible study again-man. That Bible stuff was boring, but, that's what his dad was into, since he couldn't escape it, he would endure the pain of listening to what Jesus said.

After school, James passed Joe and Joe asked, "You wanna ride with me, Ray an nem?"

"Nah, I'm cool. I'll se you tomorrow or something." The bus ride seemed long; James blamed it on him being tired. His last hour class was history, which bored him, and he had to think bout who he was going to write for an upcoming paper. He couldn't' wait to get home and go to sleep. James got off at his stop and began the three-block journey to his house. It was a cool mid spring day, James felt like it was the most boring day in the world. After he got home, he did his daily chores. Though, he couldn't understand why he had to clean all the time, he complained to his dad one time, and his dad said, "cleanliness is next to Godliness," and would look them over the rim of his glasses, and laugh. That was James' answer, and he would never ask again. He guessed, he would be closer to God then.

James woke up to his younger brother Andrew calling him. Andrew was in the eighth grade and got home an hour after James. James always thought, the younger you are, the longer you stay in school. Andrew asked James, if he wanted his after school snack their mom made for them before she went to work. He told Andrew, he was cool and began to stretch, so he could tackle his homework. While he was doing his math homework, his dad came home from work; his mom would get home late, because she worked a double shift at the hospital. His dad came into the dining-room with his usual statement: "blessings you men-blessings." James and Andrew returned a simple "what up," with a smile. His dad shook his head with a smile, and went into his study to prepare for the evenings bible lesson. On his way to his study. James said, "I need some help with this math."

His dad replied facetiously, "Did the teacher tell you how to do it?"

"Yeah."

"Does the book give you directions?"

"Yeah"

"So, why do you need me?"

"Uh, I don't know."

Forget it, what's the issue. He put on his glasses and reviewed the math problem. "O.k., what's the problem."?

"What's the answer."?

He looked at James Jr., and said "the answer is you need to start thinking, while he tapped his temple with his finger. James Sr. slid the book to him, and said, "look." He began to read the question out loud to his son. "O.k., at the end of the first quarter, the business had 3450 employees. In the second quarter, 12% more employees were hired. Now, how many employees did the business hire in the second quarter? James Sr. asked, what kind of problem is this?"

"Uh, I don't know."

"Always look at the beginning of the chapter, to determine what your doing. His dad sat down, and said, "Let's see here, O.k., it's a percentage problem. The thing about percents is, it is a multiplication problem. So when you see percentage, that means multiply. Don't worry about the story, just pay attention to the numbers." His dad began to write on a piece of paper so fast, James couldn't follow him. "Here are the numbers, 12% and the other number is 3,450 times 12. His dad asked, what would the answer be? Remember, think, said his dad.

"James said, 3,450 times 12. He calculated the math on a piece of paper and said 414."

"There you have it, said his dad."

James asked his dad, "How'd you know this?"

"You'd be surprised where one can learn." He turned and went into his study to prepare for that evenings bible study.

After his father finished preparing for bible study, he began cooking dinner. He prepared pork chops, hot water cornbread, and set out the sweet potato pie their mom made two days ago. James Sr. said, "alright gentlemen, come and get it." They ate in the kitchen. James, said the Lords prayer, and they began to eat. While eating, James asked his father what he thought about eating pork. His father responded with a 'why."

"I heard if you eat pork, its not eatin the right way."

James Sr. replied, "what does the right way mean?"

"I guess it means the way someone named Allah wants us to eat."

James Sr. laughed, and said, "Allah huh," and began laughing again. "So you've ran across someone who believes in Ol' Allah, huh?"

"I guess."

"I'll answer your question like this. "Keep livin' young man, keep livin." He laughed so hard, his eyes teared up. "Alright thanks for the question, but, in this ol' house of mine, J.E.S.U.S. is our Lord and savior- eat up so we can start bible study."

They talked and laughed about the days event, finished eating and cleared the table. It was Andrews turn to do the dishes, James cleared the homework off the dining-room table, so his dad could prepare for the bible study. James reminded Andrew, not to forget to put their moms plate in the oven. When Andrew finished the dishes, they sat at the dining-room table, waiting on their father to come from his study. James Sr. came out of the study, staring at them with a smile on his face staring at them over his glasses. James stood at the side of the table, and began to talk. James Jr., always wondered why he never sat down when he did bible study. "O.k. sirs, today's lesson is in concert with your math," he said, while pointing at James. Again, I remind you, the key word I used in that lesson was, think. To think is to formulate in the mind; it means to calculate, to weight, to judge. Open your Bibles to: Mathew 7 verse 2, it says: for with what judgment you judge, you will be judged; and with the measure you use, it will be measured back to you. He asked Andrew, what does that mean?"

"Uh, it means to think."

He pointed at James and said, "What do you think it means?"

James replied, "Your both right, you just have to expand on your answers. Let's break this down. Remember, I said to think means to judge, right?'

Shaking their heads they both said, "yep."

"Now, if we use our judgment or ability to think, then we know that is how you will be measured or weighed. Essentially, how you think, is how you will be viewed or judged by society. At the same time, were not concerned about how society looks at us, were concerned about how we view our selves. If you have negative or debased thoughts, that will reflect in your behavior. So, Jesus tells us, to use our judgment faculties, which lie in the mind. That's why, I told you to think. That means slow down and think bout what you want you read, and why you're reading it." Their father went on to speak for another hour about judging people, not from a condescending view, but from a reality of values, ethics, and moral view point. James and his brother, were always at attention while their father taught, because he was so animated, and his voice made you want to listen; also, his fathers jokes were funny, that didn't mean he wasn't serious, it meant he knew how to keep their attention.

While they were listening to their father, their mom came home from work. James Sr. said, "My sweet heart is home, so this lesson is ended due to the love of my queen. Remember, use your judgment, and start thinking, especially on your feet." James Sr. walked to their mother and gave her a hug and a kiss, and asked, "How the day in Rome went?"

His wife told him it was o.k. and began to tell him how she had to deal with some more boys getting shot and a few crazy patients, other than that, her day of being nurse patty- "with a beautiful smile,' her husband inserted. "Whelp, I made another one of my gourmet meals for you to enjoy"

"Along with my divine pie." Said, Pat.

"Hey, you want a shower or a bath? Asked James Sr.

"I'll do the shower. Hey, did the kids get in the shower yet?"

"You know the boys ain't got they funky butts in no water; don't worry, I'm on it."

As the early evening turned to night, everyone took showers, and prepared for the next day. James Sr. lay next to his wife, and talked about the lesson he gave the boys, he told her about James asking about Allah and pork. She laughed, and said "oooh wee, we might have a Malcolm X to give to the world."

"I hope not, God forbid my son sacrifice himself for a foolish people."

"Don't say that. You know black people need help with that madness going on out there. "

"Well, you know how I feel; been there done that. When we met, I told you where my life was going, and the knowledge I have is to save my self and family; now, if I reach one, I'll teach them, but all that other exposure is not necessary."

"Well don't discourage him from expanding his mind."

"When he asked me the question, I gave him my favorite line." Pat interrupted. And said, "Let me guess, keep livin'." They both laughed, sat up for a few hours talking and reminiscing about the days of Gary, Indiana and what they wanted for their two sons in the future.

Meanwhile James Jr. laid in bed, dozing off thinking about what his father taught that night. But, the thing he couldn't get off his mind, was how his father did that math so quick. And, why he always says, keep livin'. What was that all about, he never give a straight answer, James thought. Most importantly, he was going to get to the bottom of this pork, Allah thing- His dad thought that was too funny. He heard his dad laugh before, but not to where his eyes teared up. Hum, he though, as he dozed into a deep sleep.

The next morning, James work to his alarm, and the smell of his dads cheesy grits and scrambled eggs. James loved the smell of the cheese, and how it taste. The eggs were o.k., but, those cheesy grits, yumm yummm. As he began to do his hygiene and got dressed, he thought about his math class. He knew for sure that he'd get an A with the information his dad gave him He looked at himself in the six foot mirror in the corner of his room and thought, I'm so fly, he said out loud with a smile; "think

James think." He headed to the kitchen, sat down to his plate and started to eat. "I guess your too good to bless that meal," said James Sr.

"No."

"Excuse me."

"No sir." James bowed his head, and began to pray.

"I can't hear you when you head is bowed." James began reciting the Lords prayer out-loud, so his dad could hear.

It was a cool quiet summer morning, as James walked the three blocks to his bus stop. When he got to the bus stop, he noticed Joe standing there, witha slender built Puerto Rican guy with his hair pulled back into a ponytail. James walked up to Joe and said, "What up?"

Joe responded, "What up Poppy? This is my brother Sammy."

James shook hands with Sammy and, replied, "what up?"

Sammy asked, "you a Lord?'

"Nah man, I'm just lil' ol' me."

"o.k. that cool, as long as your not one of those donuts runnin around with the bullshit, they be on."

James didn't respond to the comment, but, he knew what was meant by donut, so he played it cool and asked Joe. "How come you ridin the bus?"

"I always ride the bus; I just happened to get a ride from Ray and nem'. Don't worry, you'll be seeing me all the time, I told you, the stuff with the skippin', shook me up."

"Sometimes, me and Sammy get a ride from our dad. He's usually cool, but sometimes he'll dodge us and remind us how he use to walk to school in Puerto Rico, that's just not finna happen. It was a quiet ride, it was probably due to it being early in the morning, and half the people on the bus looked as if they didn't want to be there. When the bus reached the school, Joe and James hung out at the cafeteria tables until class started, and made plans to meet up at lunch.

At lunch, they met in the rotunda where the cafeteria was. James was introduced to more of Joe's friends. Joe introduced James to everyone an began introducing them to James. "This is Jason." James took note of the pudgy middle sized frame, and the gap between his front teeth, and said, "what up."

"This is Shawn." Shawn was a tall and lanky, and played basketball for the school, he kept lots a girls around because he was on the team not because of his ball playing skills, Joe told James. Or it might be his letterman jacket, thought James.

"This is my homie from Wyoming, Steve." Steve was a short fat pudgy guy with a pig nose, and big eyes. Steve said, "what up." James nodded on response.

"This is Reggie-Reg. Reggie was a brown skinned, slender guy, with a jerry curl and freckles, he said in alight voice. "What up." Joe continued. "This Moreno thinks he Stevie Wonder or Michael Jackson or somethin'."

"Hey, Joe I told you about speaking that Spanish shit."

"Hey, its not my fault that your uncultured."

While Reggie stood looking for a response. Steve was laughing. Reggie, keened in on him. "Maaan, shutcho' fat ass up, that's why you look like Rerun from What's Happening." As the group started laughing. Joe said, "this is pretty boy Rico, if you want to get introduced to the ladies, Rico will plug you up. Rico seemed laid back; James saw why they called him pretty boy. He had a muscular build with light brown eyes, and eyelashes so dark, it looked as if he had eye-liner on. Rico chimed in. "Hol' up, all the ladies are mine. I am the ladies man, not ya'll. You gotta get your own."

Joe continued. "You already know, C, Ray, and Kev. This is Louie, the weed man, if you know someone who smokes weed, let him know, he'll plug you. James nodded. And took note of Louies laid back demeanor; he had straight hair, and his skin looked white. He found out later that Louie was Native-American, when Joe mentioned that Louie was from Cass Lake Indian Reservation, Louie called it, the Rez. The bell rang and James headed to Chemistry. James sat down, and the teacher came in and said: "Hey be quicka bout it." As the students took their seats, the teacher said. "Many of you already know me, but, for those of you who don't; My name is Mr. Miller." Mr. Miller was a short, slender white guy, with blond hair, blond eyebrows, and deep light blue eyes. James though he was wearing fake hair, because he'd never seen a white person with real blond hair. James sat and listened as Mr. Miller passed out the out-line for the class he told them there will be no homework for the class only reading assignments, and hands on testing, unless some of them had a chemistry set at home. And there were quizzes after every class, and to be ready and pay attention. Mr. Miller wrote a bunch of stuff on the board, he called atomic numbers, with a letter; he called a symbol, and said something about an atomic weight being assigned to each one. James thought, I bet my dad knows this; I can't wait to ask him, as he yawned. After first hour, James headed to his band class. He reminiscence about playing the saxophone at his old school in Gary. He sat through the class excited to learn more about music; after class, he signed for his instrument, received his reed, and he was on his way to his third hour class, study hall. It was a little boring, but, it gave him time to start reading his American history book, he still had to do research on who he'd about; damn, he thought.

The lunch bell rang; James couldn't wait to get something into his stomach. The cheesy grits and eggs wore off, all this learning made him hungry. He skipped Burger King and picked up a honey bun and a milk. He was reluctant to spend his money when he got it because every time he asked his dad for money, his dad would say something about a J.O.B. He didn't worry much about his dad, because his mom would always give him a couple dollars. As he sat down, he heard Joe say, "what up James, you going to Burger King?" James responded "nah. I'm cool."

"I'll se you in a minute," said Joe as he made his way to the back door to catch up with Reggie and the rest of the crew. James sat there eating, he took in the scenery, and wondered why the lunch room was in the middle of the rotunda, he took note that, the school seemed to be built in a circle, by the way the way the banister circled around the rotunda, yet, on the outside of the school, it looked square. His old school was definitely a square with a bunch of windows. As he sat there eating, he thought, there are a lot of different races in this school, in Gary it was almost, all black; I'm cool with whatever.

After lunch, he headed to math. He ran across Joe in the hall, so they walked to class together' Joe asked, "you wanna go to the Gardens with us this weekend?"

"What's the Gardens?"

It's the Roller Gardens, where we skate; you skate?"

"A little. I have to ask my dad an see what he says, I'll let you know." As James placed his homework in the tray on Miss Hawkins desk, he took his seat, and waited for class to start. As Miss Hawkins started to speak, James noticed she was a good lookin woman. Se was short with long brown hair, glasses, and an hour glass figure, large breast and a very nice hind end, the pretty smile was icing on the cake thought James. Miss Hawkins instructed the class about percentages, and informed them that they would have a test on that subject in two weeks. And, all homework assignments would have to be in the next day after they received them. James wouldn't know what his grade would be until the next day, so he took notes and wrote down his next homework assignment. When class was over, James went to the library to locate a historical figure to write about. He scanned the books; he couldn't find anyone he thought made a contribution to America he thought he was so important. So, he kicked back an waited until the bell rang, so he could get to history; besides, his dad could probably give him some direction, on who to write about.

After school James did the usual, chores, homework, waited for dinner, and bible study. Before bible study, James knocked on hi dads study door' "come in," said his dad.

"I need to talk to you about a history paper, I need to do."

"What does it have to be about?'

"Someone who made a contribution to America. Pointing at the bookshelf. James Sr. said, "Look on the shelf, and pick a book." James looked at the shelves and saw at least two hundred books, he asked, "How'd you get so many books?"

James Sr. Responded, "livin'."

James shook his head, and looked at the shelves, he thought the Autobiography of Malcolm X seemed like it was cool; he wondered what the book was about and headed to his room and began reading. As he read, he quickly responded to the first chapter- "Nightmare." The book grabbed his attention like nothing he had ever read. He read: "The Klansman shouted threats and warnings at het that we had to get out of town because "the good Christian white people" were not going to stand for my father's spreading trouble among the "good" Negroes of Omaha with the "back to Africa" preaching's of Marcus Garvey." He thought, damn. He'd never heard of Marcus Garvey, Klansman, or back to Africa. He guessed that's something he'll have to ask his dad, when he got around to it. In the mean time, this definitely is the book I'm using to do my report. That night his dad gave a bible study on Jesus' disciples asking Jesus, why he spake in parables; it reminded him of his dad whenever he and his brother asked him questions; for some reason, when his mom asked questions, his dad would answer her the same way, it seemed as if she got it. She would always say: " I know fat meat is greasy" or "word up." His parents would laugh and joke, that when she used it, his father would look at her and give a boyish grin, and say: "its all love baby, its all love."

Later that evening, he thought he'd ask his dad if he could go skating with Joe. His dad agreed, and let him know to be home on time.

The next morning, he met Joe at the bus stop, and told him he had permission to go skatin' on Friday. The rest of the day was like any other day at school, it was class-to-class. James was elated when he saw the A+ on his math homework. He sat in math class listening with a ken ear, and watching with a keen eye until his next class. He used his library time to read some the Malcolm X book. He read: "if you see somebody winning all the time, he isn't gambling, he's cheating. Later on in life if I were continuously losing in any gambling situation, I would watch very closely. It's like the Negro in American seeing the white man win all the time. He's a professional gambler; he has all the cards and the odds stacked on his side, and he has always dealt to our people from the bottom of the deck." Damn, that's crazy; they had it bad back then, thought James. As he read, he took note that Malcolm's mother didn't eat pork because she was a seventh day Adventist, and pork was against Mosaic dietary laws, nor did they eat flesh without split hoof, or that didn't chew cud. Hmmmm, thought James, I have to ask my dad about this.

That night at dinner, James asked his dad. "What is Mosaic Dietary Law?"

"Why?"

"In your Malcolm X book, it said, his mom didn't feed him pork because it was against Mosaic Law."

"In the book of Leviticus, it does say not to eat pork. However, you must remember, each man must worship under his own vine and fig tree."

"What's our vie and fig tree? Asked his dad.

"I don't know," responded James.

"J.E.S.U.S, and he says don't concern your self with what goes in your mouth, but, what comes out of it." James thought that made sense, and continued to eat and ponder over the Malcolm X book. James' mom interrupted his thought, whens he asked, "How's the new school?"

"It's cool, there's no windows though, and I guess they want us to pay attention in the class room."

"How's your school Andrew?"

"It's alright, I met a couple of people in my class; the teachers are alright too."

They wrapped up dinner, and prepared for bible study, James' mind shifted to roller-skating.

CHAPTER TWO

CAUTIONARY TALES

The next morning, James dressed, ate, and headed to school. On his way to the bus stop, he was thinking about the notes he had to play in first hour. Mr. Janowski, was cool, thought James. James thought, he was about sixty and had known some stuff, because he always would say, "I'm hip," but not in an old white man sense; it was sort of like his dad or his uncle Kenny would say. He wondered what was up with his Uncle Kenny. Kenny was always sayin, "what up nephew? One day your going to be like me- A playa from the Himalaya's." James' dad would interrupt, "the only thing you gonna play, is the blues when that dry game of yours doesn't work." They would laugh until they bent at the waist. Ol' Uncle Kenny, he's a trip. At the bus stop, he greeted Joe and his brother Sammy, and told them he could go skating on Friday, and he wanted to know where to meet them. Joe gave him the directions to Stardust Lanes bowling alley. It's on the right hand side, like five or six blocks from here. You can't miss it; we'll be there at seven. It was the usual bus ride, kids still waking up, or people talking about schoolwork, or their class. James was wrapped up in his thoughts, thinking about Malcolm X, and how he learned various things while growing up in Omaha, Nebraska. In first hour, he learned various notes on the saxophone, and how those notes, when played in succession with other notes, come together and make a song. Some of it he knew, but Mr. Janowski would play the songs, so James could get the feel of the music. Mr. Janowski said, "be cool and relax, it'll come to you. Never force the sound, always blow into the instrument nice and smooth, and relax." James thought, fair enough. James sat in his area, and memorized the notes, and went over them on his saxophone in the silent booth, so he wouldn't disturb the class with his sounds that sounded like a duck or a goose.

By the time lunch came around, James was thinking about his grade in math, he knew it was going to be good, and he couldn't wait to turn in his other homework assignment; besides, Miss Hawkins was someone he wanted to see before the end of the day. After lunch, he headed to math and sat in his usual seat; as Miss Hawkins placed his homework on his desk, she walked to the back of the class, James couldn't help but turn and look. He thought, damn, she sure is thick. He then turned his focus on his homework; when he saw that A+, he was elated, and thought, I can't wait to show my dad. After class, Joe walked with James and said, "I saw you lookin at that ass booooy," James responded. "Whatchu talkin about?"

"Miss Hawkins."

"Oh yeah, she is somethin' ain't she?"

"Keep dreamin Iowa boy, that's too much for you."

James laughed and told Joe he'd see him later, and headed to the library, thinkin about Miss Hawkins. As he sat reading, he wondered why a teacher would discourage Malcolm X from being a lawyer, or a doctor, and his thoughts shifted to his teacher's. He wondered, if they thought, he should be realistic about being a nigger. Hmmm, ain't that something, he thought.

He sat in history class listening to Mr. Jones booming voice. Mr. Jones was dark-skinned, and he wore square framed glasses, that were too big for his pudgy round face, he always wore sweaters, slacks, and dress shoes; he was cool, but he had this intense stare when he talked to you- he demanded attention with his eyes. James thought that was weird. After class, Mr. Jones requested that James wait, so he could talk to him. Mr. Jones said, "I saw the book you had out; what's it for casual reading or something personal?" James told him he borrowed the book from his dad for his history report. Mr. Jones replied, "That's a sincere ad great piece of work." With his intense stare, he went on "Mr. Shabazz was a great individual, and left serious foot-prints in the sand, so that leaves no room for you to muck up that history report, I expect 100% on that report; good day Mr. Blakely. As James walked away, he thought, that dude has to stop staring like that, or he will break his eyes. Oh well, I gotta meet up with Joe to go over plan's for Friday.

That night James sat in the basement practicing a song for the upcoming test. He cut it short, because he had to attend bible study. That night, his dad opened James eyes. He read from Genesis, and ran down God's promise to Abraham and how God gave Abraham descendants land from the River of Egypt, to the Great River and the River Euphrates. The thing that James focused on is, when his dad said, "I thought I'd never be teaching you this, but, since your reading about Mr. X, I'll tell you this; the woman Hagar is the progenitor of the religion of Islam. Have you gotten to where Malcolm converted to the religion of Islam?"

"No."

"Well, when you get there, remember, Islam's origins start with an African woman, named Hagar; the book won't tell you that. With that, this study is concluded-thank you sir. That evening, James Sr. talked to his wife. She commented, "Why'd you tell James that Hagar was the progenitor of Islam?"

He responded, "Reach one, teach one, sweetheart. He gave her a kiss on the cheek.

"Boy you sure know how to explain yourself."

James lay in bed dozing off to sleep, he thought; how does another religion start in the Bible? The only religion he knew was J.E.S.U.S, at least that's what his dad always said. His dad always comes up with something new. Whelp, tomorrows Friday and he'd be on some skates, he thought he went to sleep.

The next morning, James did his usual routine and headed to the bus stop. At the bus stop, he talked to Joe and his brother, the were pointing him to the bowling alley again. Joe interrupted, and said, "listen, just stop at my crib at seven, it doesn't make sense for you to get lost when I live up the street. It's the white house with the flag above the door, you can't miss it." They began to talk bout how Joe got into an argument over a foul at a pick up game at the park; "I'm tellin you, dude fouled me on purpose poppy, Joe said to his brother Sammy.

His brother's response was nonchalant. "it didn't look like it to me."

"Coooome ooon Sammy, you was right there."

With a look of disbelief on his face, Sammy responded, "Do you think I'd let someone hack you on purpose, and then walk away?"

"Alright, alright, you got me, but, I'm tellin you poppy, that mothafuckers a bum anyway; next time I'm a steal on his ass."

On the bus, Joe asked James if he played ball. James answered, "a little, me and my dad, and my brother play pick up games at the Y downtown, with some of my dads friend's from church."

Joe replied. "Man you should come play with us on Thursday."

"I'll have to see what my dad says."

At school, they talked about skatin and how it was going to be some fine girls there. The bell and everyone headed to class. The rest of the day went as usual; at the library, James took time to read some more of his book, he noticed that Malcolm X used the same slang expressions as Mr. Jamowski. James thought, cool, hip; I knew he was from somewhere else. I wonder if he knows about Malcolm X.

That night, he attended bible study, and soon after, he hurried up stairs to shower and get dressed. He gave himself a one over and thought, I look like Big Daddy Kane. James' short cropped black hair was shining, the white T-shirt, jean jacket that matched his blue jeans, along with the black and white striped shell toed Addidas; if only he could get a dookie rope that Rakhim wore in his videos, he'd really be fly. As he got to the bottom of the stairs to head out the door, his dad called him. James went to his study, looked through the double doors and said, "yeah."

"Let me look at you. Ahhh, o.k.' you tryin to look fly, ain't you?"

"It's just somethin I put together."

"Well, remember me and your uncle Kenny invented the word fly; boy, only if you know the half. Anyway, here's some money in case you want to get some snacks; and be home before ten."

"Alright. And, thanks for the money James said, as he headed to the front door. He stepped out the house into cool mid summer night; the sun was still up, so James had plenty of time to wear his summer clothes. Boy, those winters in Gary were something else, I wonder if Minnesota winters are cold like Gary's, James pondered, as he turned right at Franklin Avenue and headed to 27th, on his way to Joes house. James took note of the homes in the neighborhood and felt calmness about it as he walked to Joes house. He couldn't miss Joe's house; Joe wasn't kidding when he said it was the house with the flag in the front. The flag looked different, the only flag James remembered was the American flag. He approached the house and noticed a few bikes in the yard, and he heard a dog bark in the distance. James knocked, and a short woman with long black hair, and pretty carmel complected skin; said "yeah" in a deep Spanish accent. James asked if Joe was there. She replied "come on in; he's in the basement." As James entered the house, it smelled good, whatever was cooking James wouldn't mind tasting it and the music was different, he couldn't understand the language, but it had a nice rhythm, thought James. His thoughts were interrupted when she asked his name, and introduced her self as Joe's mom Mary.

James told her it was nice to meet her, as she escorted him to the basement. Man she's too young and pretty to be a mom. Maan, Joe's mom is gorgeous, thought James. Mary said, Joey's down there, and pointed to the slightly opened door. James ascended down the stairs and turned left to see Joe, Sammy, and two other people playin a game on Nintendo. Joe said, "what up James, you ready to bounce?" As Joe got up from the couch, he told James those were his little brother's Diego and Jimmy. Diego was about the same age as James' little brother, he looked like Joe only he was shorter, and his hair was cut low, with a tail in the back. His brother Jimmy was younger than all of them, and he just stared at James and said, "what up;" He had a cool demeanor like Sammy; they almost looked a like except Jimmy was a little chubbier. They made their way from the basement to the front door; Joe and Sammy said something in Spanish to their mom as they went out the front door. On their way to the bowling alley, Joe told James he was gonna pull a girl tonight because he looked like RUN DMC or somebody. Joe started singin "My Addidas" and making the beat with his mouth, they all laughed; as they approached the bowling alley, Joe pointed across the street at a row of light blue town houses, and told Joe that's where C lives, Ray lives across the street from the park, and pointed in the direction of the park. On the way to the bowling alley, James asked about the flag, Joe's only response was Puuertoooo Riiicoooo. As they entered the bowling alley, James saw all the bowling lanes, and to his right, was a small arcade with a few pinball machines and some video games; that's where Jason, Shawn, Steve, Reggie, Rico, Ray, Kev, C, and Louie were playing games and cracking jokes as they waited one everyone to arrive. Everybody shook. hands and headed out the side door, to the bus stop. They sat at the bus stop waiting on the bus joking, laughing, and play fighting with each other. When the bus arrived, they paid their fare, got transfers and headed to the back of the bus. As they sat there, James noticed Ray's large marker draw a five pointed star, with a cane running through it on the back of the bus seat. It wasn't anything new to James; he saw that sign many times in Gary, spray-painted on the side of buildings. As everyone talked, James took in the scenery; he noticed this bus took him two blocks from the school, and past Burger King; the ride was long, but the time passed with the guys joking, laughing, and asking each other weird questions. They finally arrived at the next stop on Hennepin Avenue, made their way to another bus stop. James asked, "Why are we waitin' here?'

"Reggie replied, "We gotta get to St. Louis Park. Here comes the bus, Reggie said over his shoulder, as he looked in the direction of the bus. By the time the other bus arrived, it was so many people, James thought, this is going to be a cramped ride. The ride wasn't that long or cramped. It was loud, and the bus driver gave out a few warnings; "there it is," said Joe, pointing at the gigantic dinosaur. They got off, and made their way to a building that looked like a big warehouse. As they entered James could feel the vibration of the music coming from the speakers, this seems more like a party than a skating rink, thought James. Joe said, Let's get you some skates." They walked past the snack counter, and a seating area to the skate counter. After James received his skates he headed to the lockers, put his shoes up and headed to the floor. Everyone skated for a little while, then began to split up; Joe, Reggie, and James were talking to some girls, while

Shawn, Ray, Jason, Kev, and Steve were by the snack counter. Rico was leaning against the lockers talking to a girl, that's when C approached them and said, "Them doughnuts are trippin, let's go." C walked off and rounded everyone up and they headed to the lockers. As everyone put their shoes on, James asked Joe what was up; ina angry tone, Joe replied, "we finna whoop some ass, that's what's up." James thought, I didn't sing up for this, damn. A bunch of guys approaching them interrupted his thought. The first guy approached them and directed his comment to C and said "Whatch yo hook ass say?" C answered the question with a punch to the guy's mouth. The next thing James knew, some carmel complected dude with a high top fade, punched him in the jaw; James heard a thud as he was hit. James backed up and did what his dad taught him to do- he threw a right and a right ducked under the punches thrown, and grabbed the guy and threw him against the lockers, and placed a fury of solid blows to his face, as fast as hands could throw them; the guy hit the floor. James began stomping on his head, cursin and yelling, while the guy tried to cover his head from the barrage of stomps to his head and face. James wasn't a stranger to fighting. In Gary, he fought a lot, besides his dad made sure he fought with the zeal of a lion; losing was not an option. The mêlée was broke up by Roller Gardens security team. The split everyone up and escorted them out the building. As they were being escorted out, the guys yelled insults at each other- Kev couldn't stop screamin' "that's why we whopped ya'll's ass mark.'" James thought whoever fought Kev had problems. Kev was too big for his age, he was over six feet, with a muscular build. As they walked to the bust stop. The St. Louis Park police were driving around. Ray said, "ya'll be cool and act like nothing happened, Louie, if you got some weed throw it." They casually walked toward the bus stop. The police car lurked, and stopped when they arrived at the bus stop; the police sat there until they were on the bus. The bus ride was a little longer, because everyone was in heir own thoughts about the fight, or they were inspecting scars and bruises from the rumble. James used the bus ride to think about the events that just unfolded, his adrenaline was still pumpin from the fight, he could go some more if the security hadn't broken it up. James pondered on the fight until he got to his stop. James entered the house before ten, changed, took a shower, and kicked back. As he layed there, he heard his dad call him. He walked down the hall to his parent's room, knocked, and heard "come in." "Did you enjoy yourself,? asked his mom.

"Yeah."

"It's good to know you can tell time," said James Sr.

"Does that mean your going to buy me a watch," James said jokingly.

"You never know what will happen in life. Alright, I just wanted to see you before you went to bed."

"Alright, good night."

Later, James lay in bed; he could feel his jaw throbbing. It was cool, whoever dude was couldn't hit that hard, he was lucky security broke it up, or it would've been worse, James thought. He turned to his side, and noticed the Malcolm X book on his night stand, he picked it up and began to read about Malcolm's life in Harlem, New York, and all the gambling and hustin he did. This dude is a trip, thought James, as he dozed off with the book in his hand.

The next morning, James woke to the sound of music; that was his dads Saturday morning routine while he cleaned the house. It sound like the Gap-Band, Early in the Morning, how ironic, thought James. He rose, did his hygiene, gathered his clothes, sheets and blankets because every Saturday was mandatory for sheets to be washed. James' dad always reminded him that, he didn't have a maid, so it was his responsibility to do his own laundry. As he headed down the stairs, he saw his dad doing the usual, on his hands and knees cleaning the kitchen floor, his dad acknowledged James with a "what up," and to go through the pantry because the floor was wet. James placed his laundry in the wash and went up stairs to start cleaning his room. His mom wasn't there, she probably had to work. He acknowledged his younger brother, who was still in bed, and told him to get up so he could do his laundry. Later, his brother came into his room, sat down on the bed, and asked, "Did you have fun at the roller gardens last night? I can't wait to go when I get old enough."

"Don't worry lil bruh, it'll be sooner than you think, now move so I can clean up. Did you put your sheets and blankets in the basement, so they could get washed?"

"Not yet."

"Well whatcha waitin on, get busy boy."

Andrew exited James' room, turned and sarcastically said, "You ain't the boss of me."

The rest of the morning consisted of cleaning, his dad sittin in his office studying, and James and Andrew throwing the football in the back yard His mom got home at 3 o'clock, his dad prepared dinner, which he called, gourmet. James asked his what he was cooking. "Food."

"You still think you're a comedian, said Patricia.

"Nah, I'm jokin', it's fried okra, cornbread, salad, and pot roast; ooohweee baby; I as thee number one chef.

"Yeah until I start cooking."

"Whelp, that might never happen, you know I don't allow Isis to lifts a finger unless she wants to."

Pat thought, it's not many men who'd treat their wife like a queen. I can hardly remember when I did anything, hell, even when I was pregnant, James was always making sure I ate right, didn't walk too far, he was even afraid to let me drive. I guess I'm lucky, two kids and a black man that's not caught up in worldly affairs. She sat and listened to James singing; early in the morning gotta find me anotha lova gotta get up in the morning to find anotha lova- gotta get up; I guess he doesn't have to be a good singer, she thought, as she laughed to her self. Pat sat on the couch listening to music until James announced dinner was ready. They blessed the table and ate. Pat announced she would be doing the dishes, because she knew they were going to the Y to ply basketball. The couple hours before the game, James sat in his room folding his clothes listening to his dad across the hall, rappn, don't push me cuz I'm close to the edge, I'm tryin not to lose my head huh, huh, huh, huh; He's a trip, thought James.

On the way to the Y, James asked his dad, "Who is Marcus Garvey?"

His dad responded excitedly, "That's the forerunner young man. Listen, Marcus Garvey is the reason why black people in America have a sense of business, and a sense of culture, and damn near everything you know about black people. He's the first brother to start a cruise ship, yeah; The Black Start Line is what it was called, until the government decided that was too much for one brotha to have. And pulled the plug, using some trumped up charged about fraud or some crap. Back then he was hangin with Nobel Drew Ali too, passes, boy let me tell you. In that time and era, for black people to be independent, and Afrocentric at the same time was something, the powers that be didn't like. We were brought to America for one thing, and one thing only; anything outside of that was not an option. Your reading Malcolm X, what did he say about being a realistic nigger? Yeah, that's how they want us. I'll tell you this, that's not an option it's good you're reading that book, its going o give you a lot food for thought."

James Sr. continued talking until they arrived at the Y in North, Minneapolis. As they entered the gym, James Sr. commented, "yeeah, getcha game faces on gentlemen, the Champ is here." They played ball for the next couple hours. James thought it was funny was funny that his dad said, "cha-ching," after he made a shot. He liked playin ball with his dad, because he would direct him to where he was suppose to be on the court; he would say, " cut, cut," Or " that's right, that's right, stay on him." After the games were over, his dad shook hands with the other men, and told them he would see them at church on Sunday. On the ride home, they talked about the games, who had the best or worst moves. When they arrived at home James Sr. reminded them, they were going to church in the morning, and to get a good nights rest. James went straight to sleep, because he was tired from playing basketball.

The next morning, James woke, got dresses, and headed to church with his family. The drive was somewhat quiet; the background was filled with gospel music on KMOJ Radio. They pulled into the church parking lot, and James saw, the usual Sunday crowd. The men and boys were dressed in their suits and ties, while the women wore skirts or dresses with short high-heeled shoes. As they crossed the street, and walked to the church, the preacher stood at the entrance of the church greeting the churchgoer's. At the entrance, they received the same greeting. "Hello, how's everybody doing this Sunday?" They took their seats in the second row, James looked around and saw the stained glass windows with doves, angels, and a person that looked as if he were praying; he always payed attention to the instruments, because that was his favorite part of coming to church- the choir. The preacher interrupted his thought, when he stood at the podium and said, "good morning everybody," in his mellow voice. The church responded in unison, "good morning." In turn, the preacher said, "God is good;" the church responded in unison, "God is great;" the preacher said, "all the time-amen?" The churchgoers responded, "amen." The preacher opened his Bible, and directed everyone to open their Bibles to the intended chapter, and said, "Today, were going to talk about Jesus on the mount being tempted by Satan-amen. The church responded, "amen." The preacher talked about verse with a high voice, then a low baritone voice, and a scream or two in between the other tones; James thought, it was interesting, but, no matter what the preacher said, James always dozed off. It seemed like he went on for hours, then he became alert when the choir began to stand up behind the preacher, and the other people that were siting in the chairs at both sides of podium. A woman stood in front of the podium, raised her hand and suddenly lowered it, and the choir belted out, " Work it out." The woman's hand went up, and suddenly lowered it again, and the choir belted in unison, "work it out; there was a few seconds of silence, then the woman raised her hand, and the choir sang in unison, "God is gonna work it out." That feels good, thought James; he sat there clappin, while others were clappin, some were doing what seemed like dancing, but, people said they had the Holy Ghost; whatever it was, made James feel good. He even had goose bumps, listening to the choir. After the choir was done, there were a few testimonies, some people had the preacher bless them with oil he would place on his pointer finger, and place it on their foreheads, and forcefully push their heads back; some were o.k., others would jump and run to the back of the church or raise their hands in the air, and say: "Hallelujah, Thank You Jesus." The offering was done, and people started to depart, shake hands, or conger grate with one another, until they walked out the door. James' parents greeted a few people, and the guys his dad played ball with, and they departed. On the drive home, James Sr. asked, if they like the sermon, everyone said, "yeah," and James Sr. responded, 'what'd you like about it Andrew?"

"The part when he got to into the argument with Satan."

"Who do you think the devil was?"

"I don't know, the red man, with long horns, and a tail."

Laughing. James Sr. said, "that's the answer, but, it's the wrong answer. See, the stories in the Bible are called allegorical tales, or cautionary tales, which means the stories have an under-meaning. It's essentially, a myth or fairy tale, but not one that's for entertainment value. These tales are termed cautionary tales, because they give you direction on what to do, or what not to do. So, when the preacher talked about the Devil, per se; he was talking about the Higher Self and the Lower Self. These two halves are always in conflict with each other. So, it's our job to know which is trying to take over, or conquer the other. James, how do you stop the Lower-Self from taking over?"

"Uh, you have to fight it, like Jesus did."

Shaking his head in agreement, while rubbing his chin. James Sr., replied, "yeah, that'll do for now, but, it's more to it than that."

Andrew asked, "how much more?"

"You have to crawl before you can walk young man.' As they drove, there was small talk about how the rest of the day would go; James' mind shifted out the window of the car, looking at other cars, a few buses, the cloud filled sky, with sun peeking through, he thought, it seems like every Sunday after church, the sun is shining even in the winter; huh, ain't that something. At the house, everyone went to their selected parts of the house to change clothes, and prepare for dinner. After dinner, James went to his room to prepare his backpack for school, and made sure his homework was in his backpack. Once everything was done, he kicked back and listened to whatever was on KMOJ.

Chapter Three

Ride or Die

After breakfast, James made his way to the bus stop. As he arrived, Joe said, "whaat, boy, you a beast with them hands socio."

James responded, "what's a socio?"

"It's a brotha, mad man."

Sammy chimed in and said, "yeah, you messed David's ass up; I looked at his face when I was getting pushed out the door, by the security, and he was fuuucked uuup."

James shrugged, and said, "man, he hit me first, I was going to stand there and let him beat me up."

Joe said, while throwing punches. "You looked like Mr. T, I pity the fool, I pity the fool."

"Man yo ass crazy." said James. The bus ride was full of Joe's excitement about Friday night. James at back, listened to him, and would shake his head from time-to-time. When they arrived at school, they met at the usual place and talked about Friday, but James was the center of attention – the bell range, and everyone went to their classes. Joe turned and said, "James meet me at the back door, we're all going to Burger King."

It was the usual morning of listening, and doing science projects, learning the songs for band, and reading in study hall. James met everyone at the back door, and they proceeded to go to Burger King. James thought, damn, it's a lot of us, I hope them dudes from the roller gardens don't show up. They walked the few blocks, cracking jokes, and shadow boxing. At the restaurant, they ordered and sat in the far corner and ate, cracked more jokes, and talk about the fight. "I'm tellin you, it was that punk Dee that started it, he's always runnin his mouth when his boy's are around, then when you see him by his self, he be like, what up all soft and shit. Dudes a bitch, next time I see him, I'm knocking his ass out, pow, straight to the kisser, said Ray.

C said, "it ain't nothing, we did what we had to do."

Anyway, interrupted Jason, what's up with Thursday?" Everyone looked at him quizzically, Jason said," Duuh, basketball."

"You know we'll be there, said C speaking for the group.

James said, I'll see what my dad says."

"Alright cool, let's get back before the bell rings." said Joe.

Ray responded, "you always tryin' to leave early, like you scared or something."

"OOOOh," said Joe as he turned and headed out the door to get back to school – the group broke out in laughter. As Joe and James entered the math class, Joe said, "ooooh chaqui, chaqui" to James. James grinned, and said, "you're a trip.' The remainder of the day went normal, library, history, and home. It was a sunny day as James walked from the bus stop, he didn't have any particular thought, in fact, he wasn't thinkin about anything, he just enjoyed the nice light breeze, and the warmth of the sun on his body. James did his chores, homework, and prepared for his dad's arrival, dinner, and bible study.

During bible study his dad went over the sermon they heard on Sunday, and spoke about the higher-self and the lower-self. James thought about Jesus representing the higher-self, and the Devil representing the lower-self. James asked, "Does that mean Jesus and the Devil don't really exist?" James Sr. looked in the air, as if he were looking on the dining-room ceiling, then looked at James, and said, "for purposes of concrete thought, yes. Essentially, my point is, that we become and embodiment of Jesus so we don't fall victim to the Devil's tricks."

"If we become Jesus' body does that mean we have to be white?" asked Andrew

James responded, "Who said Jesus was white?"

"that's what he looks like on T.V., and in the pictures at church," said Andrew.

James Sir responded, "First the word is embodiment, not body. The word means to emulate, or be an example of; secondly, if I don't tell you Jesus is white, he is not white, capice?"

Andrew nodded in agreement, and added, "So what color is he?"

"Does it matter?"

Andrew shrugged his shoulders and said, "I don't know."

"Let me know when you do. Whelp, fella's, that concludes our bible study – keep livin'."

After bible study, James practiced his saxophone for a few hours, went to his room the kick back, but he saw the Malcolm X book on his nightstand; he picked it up and began to read: I said to him I don't eat pork. James thought, I wonder if Joe knows about Malcolm X. As he read on, James was enlightened about Yacub and how Moses civilized them; the Yacubaian history placed a huge question mark on his mind, that he would find an answer for; he finished the chapter, and got some sleep.

The next morning, James asked Joe if he knew about Malcolm X. Joe responded, with a duuh, yeeah, then asked James what was up with the question. James began to tell Joe about Malcolm X not eating pork when he became a member of the Nation of Islam, and how he said a person by the name of Yaqub made white people from a brown germ in black people.

Joe told James how his dad used to tell him about Malcolm X, and referred to him as a cold dude, and how white people hated him so much, they killed him.

In shock, James said, "He's dead?"

"Yeah, I guess he had too much power, so white people paid his own people to kill him bruh."

"I guess that's at the end of the book."

"You got a book on him?"

James unzipped his backpack, and showed the book to Joe. "I'm doing a history paper, so I chose him."

"Where did you get the book from?"

"From my dad."

"Daaamn, that's dope."

"Are vice lords part of the Nation of Islam?"

"Nah, man"

"How come ya'll don't eat park?"

"Because that's law."

"What's law?"

"Vice lord law."

Sammy interrupted them and said, "The law is the Holy Divine. We don't eat no pork bruh, that's how it is; I can't tell you much about it, but Ray's Uncle used to talk about it before he went to Chicago and got locked up." They continued to talk until the bus arrived.

At school, they met everyone in the cafeteria, greeted each other, and parted for class when the bell range. It was the typical school day, James went from one class to the next, thinking about Malcolm X, why vice lords didn't eat pork, and the questions he had for his dad. After school, James gave Joe and Sammy his farewell, and headed home; I wish this sax was a little lighter, thought James. As he entered the house, he was greeted by his mom sitting on the couch. James said, "Hey mom, whatchu doin home?"

"I had an early out at work."

"That's cool," said James as he headed up the stairs to his room to put his saxophone and backpack away. James began doing his chores, when he was done, he sat next to his mom on the couch.

"Whatchu watchin?"

"I don't even know. I ain't payin' attention to the T.V., I'm tryin to relax. The T.V. is watchin me."

"Whatchu know about Yaqub?"

"the big head scientist," she said with a giggle. "I remember that, well, it doesn't go into detail in the book, but the Nation of Islam used the story of Jacob wrestling with an angel all night as proof that the white man was grafted. In the story, when Jacob's thigh was cut, or I think he ripped his leg or something like that – that portion where Jacob's leg was cut is the portion they used to show the extraction of the brown germ. The struggle between Jacob and the angel is the thought, and action of grafting the brown germ, making it lighter and weaker until it was bleached out, which would make white people more susceptible to wickedness and evil."

"So it's true that white people were made by Yacqub?"

"I didn't say it was true; remember this, if you have a group of people and you want that group to be unified, and I mean any group, you have to create an enemy so there is commonality and unity in that group, or your mission will fail. That's all the Nation did; I'm not saying they're wrong or right, I'm saying they did what they had to do to make black people conscious so they wouldn't be victims of racism, or have the self-hating mentality they had then and many have in this day and age."

"So, it's a trick to get people on the same page."

"Not necessarily a trick, I call it using wisdom to bring people together. Remember, white folks are the ones that use tricks."

James nodded in agreement, sighed, and said, "alright, I got it." James sighed and leaned deeper into the couch, and sat and let the T.V. watch him with his mom.

After his brother and dad arrived, the evening was the routine dinner, homework, bible study, enthusiastically reading the Malcolm X book.

The next morning, James arrived at the bus stop and discussed with Joe some of the things in the Malcolm X book, and the discussion carried on until they met with the rest of their friends at school. School was the norm, nothing ever exciting occurred at school thought James, the school in Gary; it was always something rowdy going on. James didn't mind because he didn't like a lot of hoopla around anyway. During math class, after admiring Miss Hawkins physique, James sat thinking about the end of the school year, but before that occurred, he had to get that history report done; he was almost finished with the Malcolm X book. With reading at home, study hall, and the library, it was going to be a quick read, besides he enjoyed the book. It was hard for him to put it down, he'd never felt that way about reading, maybe it was the fact that his mom and dad knew so much about Malcolm's teachings, not only that, they added more to what wasn't in the book – the ring of the bell snapped James out of his thought; he headed to his last hour and headed home to do the usual.

While at home, his dad asked him to go to the story, grab some milk and a loaf of bread. As James headed out the door, he walked up Franklin Avenue to the Kwik Mart instead of Dan's Market. He always liked the smell of Dominoes pizza next to the store; James grabbed the items he needed, and headed to the register. While standing there, he noticed a girl standing at the counter next to him. He thought, she's fine. He looked at her and he was surprised that she spoke first. James responded," What's up?" to her soft "hi." As James looked, he took note of her long jet black hair that stopped in the middle of her back, her dark brown eyes, thick lips, the braces; and skin, that matched the color of caramel candy. James thought, she's not black, she's mixed, damn; I wonder what she's mixed with. James paid for his items and mustered the courage to ask her name. James headed for the door a little slower than he came in, when he heard her say thanks to the cashier, he turned and said "what's your name?"

She smiled and said, "Zaria."

"Who?"

She repeated her name using syllables. "Za-Ri-Yaa."

"Oooh, o.k., my name is James. As they walked out the door, James asked if she lived in the area, she pointed in the direction of her house, and said, "I live on 25th."

They discussed where James lived, and that he was from another city, the school's they went to. James thought it was interested that Zaria went to a private school. Before they went their separate ways, James asked if he could get her number. Since neither of them had a pen, they went into the store and got one from the cashier. Zaria wrote the number on his hand, and he wrote his number on her hand. As they exited the store James promised he'd call and headed home. On the way home James thought, I can't wait to call her, and silently pronounced her name with a slight grin on his face.

Once he'd placed the groceries on the table, he headed upstairs with his dad asking for his change. He grabbed a piece of paper and a pen from his backpack and wrote down Zaria's number. He went downstairs and gave his dad his change. James Sr asked, "what was the rush?"

"Oh, I had to write this number down."

"Who's number?"

"This girl named Zaria, I just met at the store."

"Zaria, huh. Mr. Lova man. Remember, girls are complicated so be smooth and have patience; I know it's going to be hard to be like me, but do the best you can.

"Ha, yeah, alright."

The rest of the evening, James couldn't stop thinking about what he was going to say to Zaria, he missed most of what his dad said at bible study, and forgot what he was reading in the Malcolm X book, it even took him awhile to get to sleep; before he dozed off, he thought, Zaria huh. The next day, James used his time at study hall, and the library to start writing his report on Malcolm X. It was almost the end of the school year, and summer break was coming up, so he had to get the report done. He was ninety-five percent done with the book, so he could start writing.

That evening when James got home, he did the usual, with the exception of calling Zaria. He nervously dialed the number; he listened to the ring of the phone, which seemed a little longer than usual. He was in the process of hanging up the phone; he heard a soft voice say, "hello."

"uhhh, can I speak to Zaria please?"

"This is her."

"Uh, this is James."

"Hey what's up James, I was wondering when you were going to call."

"I didn't want to call at the wrong time, so I waited a few days."

"That's cool, but after today you can call anytime you want. Though, it's better if you call after five because I have cheerleader practice, it'll take me awhile to get home."

The conversation continued for an hour, as they talked about friends, family, school. Zaria did most of the talking, James wasn't much of a talker, no matter who he talked to, that's just how he was, he though. After the conversation, James hung up the phone with a smile, and said to himself, yeeah booooy. That night, James went to sleep with only one thing on his mind; Zaria. That week seemed to fly by, with school, friends, church, basketball, and the conversations with Zaria.

A week later, James approached his dad to help him with his history paper. "what's up?" James wanted him to look at his paper to see if he started it right. "Yeah, this is good, but, stick with your thoughts about the person, don't rely on the book's words, just use the information and tell the teacher how you feel about how his life contributed to society, and how his life made him a historical figure. James replied, "o.k." to his dad's advice, and went to finish his report. He sat in his room, and began to write: Malcolm X, the one who sacrificed his life so black people wouldn't have to be ashamed to say they were proud of who they were publicly, and against all odds. He wrote for the rest of the evening, and he was astonished that he could write eight pages in a few hours. He concluded, Islamic or Christianity, black people are hated equally. James took a shower, and headed to bed, that's when he heard the phone ring. He headed downstairs, picked up the receiver, and it was Zaria's voice on the other end. "Is this James?" she said.

"Yeah, what's up Zaria?"

"I thought you were somebody else, you sound different."

"Nah, I'm tired because I've been writing a history report all night.

Zaria asked what the report was about, and the conversation lasted well into the night, which James enjoyed; before they finished the conversation, James had a night planned at the movies with Zaria that Friday. The next morning was slow, James got a late start, and almost missed the bus because he stayed up talking to Zaria until eleven o'clock, he didn't mind because to talk to Zaria was worth a groggy morning. Joe commented on James' quietness on the bus, James told him about Zaria; Joe responded, "chaqui, chaquiiiii, Chico."

James gave Joe his usual response. "You a trip." James did his typical at school. He turned in his history paper with no comment from Mr. Jones, maybe he's going to wait until the last day of school, thought James. James headed home to do his chores, homework, bible study, and most importantly, call Zaria. That nights conversation was about James' and Zaria's parents. James talked about his dad and the things he taught him, Zaria responded, that her dad worked for Honeywell and he worked a lot. Her mom worked for 3M, so they didn't have a bible study, and if they went to church, it was on Easter with her Grandma. As long as she got good grades, she didn't have any issues with her parents. James also found out that her dad was from India, and her mom was white. James thought, that explains her complexion. She told James about her friends, and how she liked the school she went to. The conversation went well into the night. After they were done talking, James went to bed, thinking about Friday at the movies with Zaria.

That Friday morning, he told Joe that he couldn't make it to the roller gardens, because he was going to the movies; besides school was almost out, and he could spend time with him then. Friday evening came, and James stood in front of the mirror admiring his sense of style, and the fact that he looked fly in his black jean jacket, black Levi's, white T-shirt, and his Adidas. He said goodbye's to his family, and headed out the door. It was a nervous walk, but he had to do it; he arrived at her home, rung the bell, and Zaria answered with a smile and told him to come in. As he entered the house, he noticed it was well kept, the furniture was leather, and the carpet was thick and soft. Zaria told him to follow her so she could grab her purse. They went to her room, and James took note of the Michael Jackson poster; the other's he didn't know. James asked, "who is that?" pointing at a poster.

"Oh, that's The Jets. You never heard of The Jets?"

"Nah."

"They're from Minnesota." James stood there with a blank look on his face. Zaria sighed and said, "come on, before we miss the bus." They walked and talked as they headed to the bus stop; James had never been downtown, so he enjoyed the ride, and the talk with Zaria. They got off and transferred to another bus that let them off in front of the Skyway Theater. They went in and bought tickets to see Driving Miss Daisy. James thought the movie was good for Zaria's sake since she picked it. She said she saw it in the newspaper or something. James wasn't much of a movie guy, besides, he didn't see the point in watchin an old black dude drive a naggin old white lady around. Since he enjoyed being with her, he sat there, ate his popcorn, and watched the movie. After the movie, they went to A Slice of New York, ordered pizza and discussed the movie; James nodded in agreement with whatever Zaria was talking about. As they left the restaurant, Zaria turned and pointed in the direction of a bridge, and said, "My school is across that bridge." James looked in the direction she was pointing, he noticed a group of guys standing in front of an arcade, his heart jumped. He noticed it was David, and some of his friends from the roller gardens, damn, thought James. He told Zaria it was cool, turned and headed to the bus stop. James walked at a brisk pace, so he could put as much space between him and David as possible. As they stood waiting for the bus, he hoped David stayed at the arcade until he got home. Before the bus arrived, Zaria said, "why you want to go home?"

"Uh, my dad wants me to be home early because we have some stuff to do in the morning."

"Oh, because I could show you around downtown, me and my friends come down here all the time – you like video games?"

"They're cool."

"good because Pops Arcade is right down the street." So, that's the name of the place huh, James thought. Zaria interrupted his thought, by telling him about the City Center, the book store, and that the people at Pops won't let kids in until after six o'clock because kids skip school and hang out in there; she gave James a geographical tour of downtown until the bus came. Phew, he thought, when the bus arrived. On the ride home, he and Zaria talked about what they would do the next time they went out together, James told her he would have to ask his dad, but, he was thinking, I hope its not downtown.

Their stop arrived, James walked Zaria home, and told her he would call later. On the walk home, James thought about David, and how he got into that mess. He figured as long as David didn't live around the neighborhood it wouldn't be any more problems.

At home, his dad asked how his trip to the movies went. James told him about his night out with Zaria, after they finished talking, James took a shower and went to bed.

The next morning at the bus stop, James told Joe and Sammy about seeing David at Pops Arcade. Sammy said," Why were you down there, that's where them punks be all the time." James explained that he was with Zaria at the movies and he saw him. Joe said, "man bruh, when you go down there be careful, that's where everyone goes, it's wide open down there. James thought, the next time he goes down there, he'll keep his eyes open. The rest of the day was normal. James received an A on his paper, it looked like this semester, James has all A's, it felt good to show his parents that he was doing good in school.

The bell rang, and that was it until September, no more school. James and Joe sat on the bus making plans for the summer. "You gotta come to the games on Thursdays." Said Joe.

"I'll see if I can make it." James' mind was on Zaria, and hanging out with her for the summer. That evening James did the usual, the only thing that was different was no homework. Later in the evening before James called Zaria, his dad told him he'd have to get a part time job, James though, that's cool, and headed for the phone. The conversation lasted until late in the night, but James didn't have to go to school, so he and Zaria made plans to meet at her house the next day. James sat and watched T.V. until he went to sleep. The next morning, his dad woke him up for breakfast. James reminded him that he didn't have to go to school. His dad said, "you gotta get up out that slumber, a lazy body makes a lazy mind; do your chores and find something to do."

After James' dad left for work, James did the dishes, cleaned his room, and turned on the T.V.. That afternoon, he went to Zaria's and they talked for a couple hours, then they headed to a restaurant called Big Olaf's. James saw the restaurant whenever he would go to the store. They entered the restaurant and stood at the little counter to order.

James ordered a hamburger and ice cream that sat in a sweet waffle shell, Zaria ordered the same. James thought, this place is nice, it reminded him of the restaurant on the T.V. show Happy Days with the small red booths, minus the old school music – he and Zaria sat there eating and talking about James finding a job, and what type of job he would get. She told him, how she dreaded the day she would have to get a job. But, the cool thing about him having a job is she could pick him up to go to work, and pick him up from work. Zaria was in the 11th grade, so her parents promised her she would have access to one of the cars, because she could her driver's license a few months ago.

James thought that was cool, and expressed that idea to Zaria. After they ate, they sat there for awhile chattin and laughin, Zaria thought James was cool because he made her feel happy and giggly; besides, he was laid back and easy going, his dark features and his slender muscular frame made him a total package, she thought, with a smile. It was getting late in the afternoon, and James made plans to be at Joe's house. He walked Zaria home and headed to Joe's. It was a cool day, it was getting hotter because the warm, cool spring was turning into a hot, cool summer; James didn't mind because he never got used to the winter. As he approached Joe's house, he looked at the flag, and thought, they're serious about Puerto Rico.

He knocked, and Joe's dad let him in, and told him in a deep Spanish accent that Joe was in the basement. James headed to the basement, they sat talking and joke around until five-thirty; James had to get home for supper and bible study. That evening, James' dad asked him what he did with his day. James explained his trip to Zaria's and Joe's. His dad reminded him to be at home and on time for bible study, James thought this would be the best time to ask his dad about Thursday basketball games. His dad's response was a yes, but not to forget his Saturday night games with him and his brother. They sat and ate dinner with the usual questions and answers, most of the questions surrounded him and Zaria's relationship. His dad asked if it was serious. James responded that he didn't know.

James Sr. teasing him said, "You ain't in love is ya boy?"

"Nah"

"I don't know, I can see the sparkle in your eye, spaarkaliiin in your eeeye."

Everyone laughed and continued joking about James and Zaria. After dinner, James did the dished and called Zaria. The next morning James got up at his usual seven o'clock because his dad was going to wake him up anyway; they ate breakfast, after his dad left for work, James decided to do some laundry. After he was done, he sat back and watched a few game shoes with his brother Andrew. That afternoon, James headed to Joe's, they sat around talking and playing video games; they decided to got o C's house and see what he was up to. C's house was a block away – C's little sister answered the door with "what ya'll want?" Joe said, "Don't worry about it little girl," as he moved her to the side. They headed to C's room; when they entered, they saw C and Ray sittin back talkin.

"What's up bruh?" said Joe.

As they shook hands Ray responded, "aw nothin Lord. What's up James?"

"Same ol' thang," said James as he thought about C's room having a lot of comic book characters on the walls. James said, "You into comic books real deep huh?"

"Yeah man, that's what I liked to do in my spare time." Said C as everyone at the spare time comment. James sat in a small wooden chair from the kitchen as they discussed what they were going to do for the summer. Ray said, " I know one thing, I'm gonna do something nasty to Cassandra. C responded, "She's a tease with all that not right now Ray. What's up with her friend Jennele, she's fine; I'd love to get some of that."

Ray responded, I'll ask and see what's up on Thursday. What's up, you gotta girl James?" Joe interrupted," Yeah, he got one, he keeps her hidden though." They all laughed and James told them about Zaria. "That's cool," said C, "it's better than not having anyone, at least you gotta shot bruh." They sat around the house that afternoon discussing girls, their figures, body times they liked, and disliked until it was time for James to go. James headed home for dinner and bible study. That evening's bible study was based on a verse from Proverbs, his dad repeated the verse twice. "Listen to counsel and receive instruction, that you may be wise in your latter days." His dad explained the verse and gave a few examples because Andrew didn't seem to understand what his dad was saying. James thought he was talking about him getting a job this summer. After bible study, James headed for the phone to call Zaria, as they were talking, James Sr. called James to his office. He stood in the doorway, as his dad asked him, "You read Malcolm X, right?"

"Yeah."

Handing him a book, he said, "here's something that will place a better perspective on the teachers he taught." On his way back to the phone, he looked at the title; The Black Book the True Political Philosophy of Malcolm X. His dad reminded him to read that book over the summer, because it wasn't good to have your mind voice of knowledge.

He picked up the phone, "Hello."

"Yeah, I'm here."

"Oh, my dad gave me this book to read."

"I was just sittin here waitin. What's the book about?"

"Malcolm X."

"That's cool." James told her how he got an A on his history report, then switched the conversation to what they were going to do tomorrow. They couldn't figure it out, since Zaria had her mom's car, she said she would come get James at one o'clock and they'd figure it out then. After the conversation, James went to his room, laid back, and look at the cover of the book, thinking, that's what he looks like, he looks like a drawing on the other book, but the picture of him is better. I'll get into this tomorrow. He took a shower, kicked back with Zaria on his mind, while listening to Late Night Love on KMOJ.

CHAPTER FOUR

LOVE AT FIRST SIGHT

The next day, James heard a knock at the door, it was Zaria. She looked lovely as ever in her fitted jeans and red top that complimented her breasts, James thought, hmmm, she is too much. He looked at her smiling, and invited her in. "This is a nice house."

"Thanks. Oh, this is my little brother Andrew." Andrew looked up from the picture he was drawing and said, "what's up." They left and got in the car. James thought, this is nice, as he leaned back in the dark blue Volkswagen. Zaria drove to Minnehaha Falls, James had never been there. They stood and watched the water fall over the cliff with a big woosh; Zaria said, "me and my friends come down here all the time."

"Yeah, this is nice."

"Come on," Zaria said, as she grabbed him by the hand and escorted him down some stairs to a small bridge, where they could watch the waterfall from a different angle. "This water empties into the Mississippi River," as she pointed in the direction of the water flowing. "It's amazing isn't it? In the winter, the water freezes in place. So what's up Mr. James?" Zaria said as she hugged him around the waist.

Looking deep into her eyes, in a smooth tone, he said, "I'm chillin."

"You always chillin." Zaria said with a grin as she looked up at him. "You gotta girlfriend?"

"Nah."

"How come?"

"I don't know, maybe I'm not cool enough."

"You looking for one?"

"It depends if she wants to be one."

She gave him a light slap on his chest and said, "Noooo, seriously, are you lookin for one?"

"Yeeep."

"So whatcha think about me being your girlfriend?"

"That's cool."

"So we're a couple then?"

With a smirk on his face, James said, "Since I'm not busy why not."

"Come here" said Zaria as she lightly held James' face steady so she could kiss him. Zaria looked James in the eyes and smiled, then turned around so he could wrap his arm around her from behind. They stood there for a few minutes, each in their own thoughts about what had just occurred. Zaria then escorted James up some stairs to a small bridge overlooking the falls talking about how the water flowed so fast, but looked so harmless – they spent the next couple hours exploring parts of the park across from the waterfall. They decided to buy ice cream at the Dairy Queen in the distance. They sat in the car and ate Blizzards, talked, when they finished, they headed to James' house so he could get home before dinner. As James waved goodbye to Zaria, he entered the house and saw his mom sittin on the couch, letting the T.V. watch her. "What's up Mrs. Blakely?" said James as he plopped down on the couch next to his mom.

"Oh, I'm o.k., just sittin here letting this T.V. watch me. Who was that?"

"Who was who?"

"The whoever, who was in the car that dropped you off?"

"Oh, that was who was Zaria."

"She gotta car?"

"Nah, that's her mom's car, she lets her use it since she has her license."

"Oh, o.k.. Where you guys go today?"

James explained how he and Zaria went to the falls, and hung out at Dairy Queen for awhile. "Oh, that's nice." They continued to talk until James' dad came home and prepared dinner for the family. While at the dinner table, James' dad asked James if he'd started the book he gave him. James told him not yet, his dad reminded him he had until the end of the summer, but not to rush. He reminded him of the importance of acquiring knowledge so it can be applied throughout his life, and the same went for Andrew. After bible study, James called Zaria to see what was on their schedule for tomorrow, Zaria told him; she'd pick him up. They talked for a couple hours, Zaria did most of the talking; boy this girl has a lot to say, thought James. He didn't mind, after all, he didn't have nothin to talk about. James headed up stairs to relax, and ponder on the thoughts that were running through his mind; he looked and saw the book his dad gave him on the nightstand next to his bed. He picked it up and started reading, then thought, how does standing up for black people's rights spell anti-American, it's strange when most American's think of Malcolm X, they think of him as un-American or anti-American. He read a few more pages and dozed off.

The next day, Zaria came over, and she drove them to Minnehaha Falls, they talked, joked, laughed, kissed, and hugged; James felt good when he was around Zaria. After they hung out at the falls, they headed home. They sat in front of James' house talking and listening to music – James saw his dad pull up behind them, he got out, walked over, and said, "What's up? And your name is?"

"Oh, his I'm Zaria."

"Nice to meet you, my name is James, I'm the refined version of this James. So, you're the one my son spends his time with."

"Uh, I guess."

"O.K., that's cool. I gotta go, ya'll be good, and it was nice meeting you Zaria."

They continued to talk for a little while longer, James gave Zaria a kiss, and told her he'd call later because he had to go to the park and play basketball. That evening, James went to Joe's house, and they walked to the park. James noticed the park wasn't far from his house. They talked and joked on the way to the park. Once they arrived at the gym, James was picked on a team that didn't look too athletic; the game was to twenty-one with no two-point field goals. James played the small forward position, which Shawn played; Shawn was tall and skinny with no agility, or basketball I.Q., he was just tall. He was a good passer, and his handles were incredible, it looked as if James were playing with amateurs – James learned how to play basketball when he was six years old; that's all his dad did was put a basketball in front of him, besides, his uncle Kenny played for Indiana State so basketball was second nature to James. He used to play for the schools he went to and local park boards, but he wasn't interested in playing ball, he did it to make his dad and uncle Kenny proud of him. Now, he just played on the weekends, that was good enough for him. James pump faked, Shawn jumped passed James, James kept going and did a reverse lay up to win the game, "Cha-chii-ing!" said James as he landed. There were a lot of oooh's when he made that shot. James said excitedly, "Who got next?" They played until the gym closed. As they walked through the park, Joe told James, "Man, you should play for the school."

"Nah, I'm cool, I just play for fun."

"Bruh, you're good; you were shakin and bakin Shawn the entire time and he's a starter for the school.

"Nope, I don't play for schools, or leagues, I just play for fun."

They stopped at the corner, said their goodbyes, and made plans to get together tomorrow for a house party at Cassandra's house. James acknowledged he'd be at the party and headed home. As he walked home, he enjoyed the early summer evening and the serenity of the neighborhood, though it felt good, at the forefront of his mind was Zaria. When he made it home, he took a shower, found a snack, and headed for the phone – they talked for a few hours and made plans to see each other tomorrow afternoon because he had to meet Joe at his house later in the evening.

The next afternoon, James and Zaria met and she drove him downtown, so they could walk around the City Center and talk. On the ride downtown, James could only think of running into David or any of his friends. They parked in a parking lot across from the City Center. James immediately looked in the direction of Pops Arcade to see if his nemesis was hangin out, he didn't notice anyone, so he proceeded across Hennepin Avenue. They went into the semi-crowded mall, walked around and window shopped for awhile until Zaria asked, "Do you like potatoes?"

"I don't know, I guess." James thought the question was weird as he followed her to a restaurant, called One-Potato-Two-Potato. She ordered them potatoes with cheese, sour cream, and bacon bits; James declined the bacon bits, and ordered a deluxe potato, he didn't know what was on it, he hoped it had enough stuff on it to cover the potato. They sat at the table in the rotunda in the middle of the other restaurants overlooking 5th Street. They ate and talked until late afternoon, and headed back to South Minneapolis. On the drive back, James thought, I have to get familiar with the city so I can avoid downtown altogether, or find another location downtown to go with Zaria. Zaria dropped James off at his house, they gave each other a huge and a kiss as they departed. James read a chapter of the book his dad gave him, and thought, there's more to Malcolm X than he thought. He went to sleep until dinner, got up, ate, went to bible study, and headed for his room to get dressed for the party. He did the usual once over, admiring himself in front of the full length mirror, thinking, I see why Uncle Kenny gave me this mirror, just like he said, it makes you look fly. James headed out the door and walked to Joe's house. He was greeted by the flag hanging over the entrance of the house. He knocked, and Joe answered with, "what up?"

"It's party time," said James. Joe turned and said something to his dad in Spanish. They walked to the bowling alley to meet everyone. When they entered the bowling alley, James saw: Jason, Shawn, Steve, Reggie, Rico, Louis, Ray, C, and Kev. They greeted each other, and Ray said, "let's ride ya'll." They departed and headed to the back of the bowling alley parking lot. They got in two separate cars, James got in the back seat of a light brown Chrysler. As they drove, they listened to rap music, and James could smell Louie's contribution to the group, James decline a hit of the joint, and rolled down the window so he could let the smoke out of the car. They arrived at a white house with an enclosed front porch, went in and greeted everyone; James was introduced and he began looking around. It was a nice place, in the living room, there were some girls sittin on a tan couch drinking beers out of plastic red cups, in the dining room were people sittin at a table playing a game called quarters. This is cool, thought James. He was offered a beer, and Joe introduced him to a few more people in the house; Ray said, "This here is off limits, bruh," as he pointed at Cassandra sittin on his lap. Cassandra was nice, she had dark brown, neck length hair, hazel eyes, and her skin was bronze colored, she wasn't mixed, but her butt was a lot bigger than a lot of girls at the party and that he'd seen, no wonder why she's off limits, thought James. James said "Hi," and went and watched the dice game in the kitchen.

There were a few people sittin at the kitchen table playing spades, he wasn't introduced to, that's when Kev looked up at James and said, "Hey James, that's chief right there," pointing at a stock, well built dark-skinned man with a bald head. "What's up? Don't call me chief though, my name is Vino, they call me V." "Anyway," interrupted Kev, pointing at the other people at the table. "That's Cedric, Ken, and Lord Fred. The older brotha's. Lord Fred said "What up bruh?" with a nod. "How long you been a brotha?" Before James could say anything, Kev looked up from the dice game and said "he ain't no brotha, he's seeking though."

"Oh yeah, o.k.," said Lord Fred. "Holla at us when you make up your mind to come home James." James nodded in agreement, and went to find Joe; James found Joe at the dining-room table playing quarters; he must've been pretty good because he wasn't doing too much drinking. As the night wound down, people were sittin around talkin, playin spades, shootin dice, and playing quarters. James sat talking to a girl named Michelle, everyone called her Chelle. As James sat talking to Chelle, Ray said, "Let's bounce ya'll, so we can get some food." They departed saying "mighty" and headed to the cards. Ray asked C, "What car you want?"

C responded, "I'll drive the black one." Ray jumped in the light brown one. They packed in the cars, James sat in the back seat of a black Jeep Cherokee that C was driving, they pulled off and headed to McDonalds listening to Rakhim reciting the lyrics: I use to hol' up, fol' up, don't smile cuz don't nothing move but they money. They drove about four blocks, turned right on Lake Street, it had to be ten seconds, that's when James saw the police lights flash on the car Ray was driving> He saw Ray speed past the car he was in heading up Lake Street. Aw shit, thought James.

That's when C turned down the music, sped up, turned right on a side street, and floored the gas. They were two blocks away from Lake Street when a police car seemed to come out of nowhere and jumped behind them with sired blaring. C wouldn't stop. He seemed to go faster as they led the police car several blocks. Joe said, "Hurry and turn before more cops come." C jerked the vehicle right, pushed the gear shift in park, and hit the brakes. James could hear the car gears rattle and grind, as C said "Run." James jumped out of the car as it was still moving, as his foot hit the street, the momentum of the car forced him to stumble forward, so he rolled, but it seemed like the roll pushed him into a full run, all he knew that he was running into someone's yard full speed. James hopped a fence and started sprinting. All he heard was sirens but he couldn't see any police cars. HE kept running through yards to keep cover so he wouldn't be seen by the police. The next thing James knew, he was in a yard looking at the back door of the McDonalds. James stopped to catch his breath and dust off his clothes. He calmly jumped over a fence, walked across the parking lot, and into the side door of the McDonalds. He stood there and gathered himself, and asked the cashier if they had a bathroom. She pointed him in the direction of the bathroom. James went into the bathroom, and looked at himself to see if he was dusty, he looked in the mirror and thought to himself, these dudes are crazy. I gotta get home. As James exited the bathroom, he could see police cars driving around canvassing the area, he reckoned they were looking for him. He decided to order some food and sit in McDonalds for a little while, or at least until there were no police cards around. He ordered a big Mac, fries, coke, and an apple pie and found a place to sit away from the windows. He ate slow and planning how he would get home, he thought, the bus that went up twenty-seventh was his best option. If he walked he might get spotted, besides that bus would let him off closer to his house. Once he saw the heavy police traffic die down, he saved some of his food, and headed out the door. He turned right on Lake Street, and began walking to the bus stop. He sat on the bus bench thinking, the bus was taking too long, he let out a huge sigh when the bus arrived ten minutes later. He sat in front f the bus, and slouched down, so he couldn't be seen. When the bus arrived at his stop, he was a little calmer, but he still walked a little faster than usual. He entered the house and his brother Andrew greeting James with a "what up?" James acknowledged him, and asked if he wanted some McDonalds and gave him the apple pie and fries while he finished his hamburger. "Zaria called, she wants you to call when you get in."

"Alright," said James as he headed up the stairs to change clothes and take a shower. After his shower, he thought it was too late to call so he decided to call her in the morning. That night James went to sleep thinking about how crazy his night went.

The next day was normal, he and Zaria went out to a local restaurant, ate, talked, and decided to go to her house and hang out for awhile. They sat in her room listening to music and talking until James changed the radio station to KMOF; "Why'd you turn from the station?"

"That music is wack, this is soul music girl. You never heard of James Brown, Zapp, or The Gap Band?"

"No."

"You don't know what you're missing!" said James while he did some of James Brown's footwork – "owwwww." Zaria smiled and pulled James onto the bed, so he would be on top of her, and give him a deep passionate kiss. James pressed his lips against hers and returned the passion. James felt her tugging gently at his shirt pulling it up over his head to get if off; soon after, they were both undressed, in bed facing each other like adults, though this was James' first time, their bodies were movie together like waves in the ocean. "Don't stop, don't stop, don't stop." Said Zaria as she shivered and erupted like a volcano. Since they would be alone for a few hours, they lay in bed giving each other passionate kisses and exploring one another's body. James suddenly lay awake, he noticed Zaria lying next to him; he thought, I guess it wasn't a dream, and smiled to himself. He gently woke Zaria up, and told her he had to leave before her parents got home. She responded with a smile, and gave James a hug. They both dressed and headed for the car so Zaria could drop him off.

They hugged and kissed before James exited the car and made plans to meet later. James entered the house to the smell of his dad making roast beef and cabbage, James was famished, he greeted his dad, went up stairs, took a shower, and changed clothes. That evening at dinner, they discussed James getting a job, and how far he had gotten in the book; it was the usual knowledge packed dinner discussion, though being responsible was the under-tone of the discussion. James was starting to get what his dad talked about, for some reason it hit him and he would think, oooh, o.k.. After dinner, James sat and read until bible study, after bible study, he followed up on his plan to call Zaria. Zaria asked about the party James went to. "It wasn't a party, it was more like a gathering of friends. It was cool though." He made sure not to tell her about the eventful night of a high-speed chase with the police. They talked for awhile and decided to hang out the next day. James hung up the phone and watched T.V. until he went to sleep.

The rest of the week was cool, he and Zaria got together and continued their passionate escapades. He, his brother, and his dad attended their regular basketball games, and Sunday church was definitely in the Blakely family schedule, at least the choir was there, thought James.

Meanwhile, James continued to hang out with Joe and the rest of the crew. One day while at Joe's house, they made plans to go to a house party; James agreed he would attend minus the stolen cars. Since the party was on a Friday, it fit into James' schedule. He hung out with Zaria until Friday – when Friday came, he met at Joe's house, and they walked the four blocks to the Lake Street bus stop. James asked where the party was. C responded, " It's up on Grand." The bus arrived, they got on, and headed to the party; they laughed and joked until their stop. They got off and headed toward the house, as they entered the house party, a guy at the door waived a hand held metal detector over each of them, they paid the six dollars to get in; James looked around and saw that whoever threw the party basically removed all the furniture in the living room and dining room. The kitchen door was blocked by a table that served as a makeshift bar, there was a couple kegs and some hard liquor for a dollar a cup. James passed on the drinks and opted to lean on the wall watching everyone else. They were in the party about an hour when James heard, "what up folk, what up G?" He turned to see who it was, and his heart jumped, and he thought, damn. He tapped Ray on the shoulder who was standing next to him drinking and talking to a female. Ray looked in the direction of James pointed and said, "shit bruh." Ray stood there for a second, and went to gather his friends so they could leave without being noticed. James followed suit, and found Louie selling weed to someone, he whispered in his ear about what he saw and Louis immediately said to the person who wanted to purchase the weed, "hol' up, let me talk to my boy for a second." They turned and walked toward where everyone was standing with their backs against the wall. They stood there trying not to draw any attention to themselves, Rico said, "What's up ya'll, what we gonna do, stand here and wait for them to notice us or leave?"

Ray said, "Let's bounce cuz it's too many donuts in here." As they walked toward the door, one of the G.D.'s named Robbie said, "What's up hook as nigga," to Ray. There was a pause as James and his friends looked at each other with an uh, ooh, response. That's when David threw the first punch, and the melee ensued. James did what he knew best, throwing lefts and rights as fast and as hard as he could. He could see Ray and Joe fighting David. Rico and Jason had their backs against the wall throwing punches at Dwayne and Chris. James was hit in the head with a blow that stumbled him, he grabbed the person and he could see it was the guy from the door with the metal detector. As they fought, Ray said, "Let's get out of here." They fought their way to and out of the front door. As they got outside, Joe said, "Come on ya'll." They ran down to the street and James saw Joe running into the yard Joe had to a piss in before they made it to the house party. James followed, that's when he saw Joe grab something out of the bushes and ran back to the front of the house, as James was trailing him, he heard pop, pop, pop, pop. James realized Joe was shooting at the people they were fighting. "Come on man, let's go!" yelled Rico. They ran three blocks, but they passed the bus stop, James didn't know where he was going so he followed everyone else. Then he heard the sirens. "Here they come ya'll. Let's split up and meet at Zantigo's by the bridge," said C. As they split up, James followed Joe and Louis, they ran until they got to Zantigo's restaurant. They went in, ordered some food, sat down, and waited for everyone else to show up. C said, "We should go, if we keep waitin, ain't no tellin if the police or them donuts gonna show up." They sat and discussed their options, that's when James noticed the phone booth at the corner across the street. James said, "I'll be back," and went to the phone booth. When he came back, they asked who he called, James responded, "I got someone to come pick us up." They sat in the restaurant for about forty minutes and James saw Zaria walk through the door of the restaurant. She saw him and waved with a smile, James told everyone, "let's go." Everyone got into the car, James turned to Joe and asked, "you don't have that do you?"

"Nah, we're good bruh."

"Where we goin?" asked Zaria. James gave her the directions to Joe's house. The drive was somewhat silent; Zaria asked, "What's up with the party?"

Joe responded, "It was raided by the police." Everyone sat back and ruminated on their own thoughts about the incident while Zaria drove to Joe's house. At Joe's house, Joe, Louis, and C got out, said their goodbyes and made plans to meet tomorrow afternoon at Joe's. Zaria pulled off. While driving, Zaria said, "You're kind of quiet."

"You know I'm the silent type."

"Mmmhmmm, that sounds good."

James leaned over and looked at Zaria with a smile, "Oh yeah."

They drove to Zaria's, went in, and she told James that her parents would be for another hour, so they could hang out for a little while she squeezed on James' bicep. Zaria pulled James close to her so she could give him a kiss, as she caressed the back of his head, she felt a bump. "What's this?"

"Oh nothin, just a bump."

"This is a big bump, were you fightin?"

"It's nothing, it'll go down in a couple days."

Zaria sighed and said, "Oh my goodness." And they began to feel each other's pleasures for the next hour. Zaria dropped James off at his house, and made plans to see him the next day, he reminded her it would a little later because he had to go to Joe's, so he'd call her to come over.

The next day, James left his house that afternoon to head to Joe's. It was a slow walk because he was tryin to figure out how all this stuff was happening so fast; he'd figure it out, he thought. When he got to Joe's house, they headed to the park by the basketball court and sat. James saw everybody that was at the party, but, there weren't any smiles or laughs. They sat and discussed the prior evenings event, everyone wondered how the other person got away without being arrested or being shot. During the discussion and retaliatory comments about David and his crew, Ray asked James, "What's up James, you in? You should be if you're not. They think you're with or one of us. You might as well make the move and be affiliated with us. If you ride with us, we'll ride with you. You gotta do something because you gotta target on your back bruh."

James pondered on it for a few seconds and said, "as long as I don't get in no mess with stolen cars, I'll ride." They all laughed at the stolen car comment, and told him they'd take him to rotation on Friday so he could be blessed in. They sat there that afternoon talking and deciding what they were going to do that day. James told them he was going to Zaria's, Joe interrupted, "Boy she is fine as hell ya'll."

Ray asked, "You getting some James?"

"You never know." James said as he smiled, turned, and walked towards Zaria's house.

That Friday James went to Joe's house, and they headed to Chelle's to meet everyone. Once they got to Chelle's, they sat around for awhile, and head to Vino's. Vino lived about three blocks away. He was older than James, James thought he was twenty or twenty-one. It was obvious he wasn't in high school, and he didn't hang with them. They arrived at Vino's and everyone headed to the basement; James was told to wait in the living room. He sat on the couch thinking, what are they up to, I hope it's not trouble, his thought was interrupted by a white woman with long black hair, blue eyes, and very top heavy, with tight blue jean shorts on and a tank top. She said, "hi, my name is Jan, what's your name?"

James sat looking astonished at her body and looks and said, "My name is James." His answer came out squeak because his throat had become dry while looking at her. James sat there talking to Jan trying not to concentrate on her breasts pressing against the fabric of the tank-top, he tried not to look, but he couldn't help it. So he looked at his hands on his lap. About a half hour had passed, and Joe told James to come in the basement. Once James arrived at he basement, he was told to stand in the circle, Vino asked him if this is what he wanted to do. James responded with a yes. Vino gave James instructions to hold his hands up with both palms and repeat after him. James repeated the oath after Vino – After James finished reciting the oath, everyone gave him a hug and taught him the handshake they all did when they greeted each other. It was official, James was blessed in as a member of the Vice lord Nation. He couldn't describe how he felt. He hung with these guys all day, but it was a different feeling. He looked at everyone and thought, It's like love at first sight.

CHAPTER FIVE

THE HOLY DIVINE

B rotha's" had a nice ring to it, as James repeated the word to himself. As they sat around the playin pool and talking, Vino pulled James to the side and discussed the importance of learning the literature, rules, and prayers that were essential to the organization. James liked the way Vino talked, and the words he used to explain things to him, I could learn a lot from him, James thought. After he talked to Vino for a while about the ends and outs of being a vice lord, it reminded him of the things Malcolm X spoke of when he was a member of the Nation of Islam; as he and Vino departed with a hand-shake, Vino wrote his number down and told James he could call anytime he had questions. After rotation, everyone was going to Chelle's house for a get together, James declined because he had a meeting with Zaria.

James headed to Zaria's house with thoughts of touching and holding her, Mmmm, he thought as he walked. When he got to Zaria's, he was surprised to be greeted by a short pretty, petite white woman, with long black hair and wide Chinese cut eyes; she looked like a miniature version of Zaria, only her skin was lighter. She greeted James with a handshake and said, " I was wondering when I would get to meet you, my name is Ann." She waived James further into the house and told him to have a seat, as she called Zaria to let her know James was there to see her. Zaria came into the living room with a smile and said, "heey babe."

James responded with his usual, "what up."

Zaria teasing James said, "you look nervous, its not because my mom is here is it?" leaning deeper into the leather sofa James, responded, "nah, I'm cool."

Zaria whispered in James' ear that they couldn't go upstairs, as she lightly pinched him. James smiled and said, "oh wooow." Zaria escorted him to the back of the house, so they could sit on the glass enclosed patio. James thought, it had a nice open airy feel, the furniture seemed to swallow James up as he leaned into the sofa. Zaria said, "are you going to tell me about your head or what?"

"N-0."

"Why not?"

"Why?"

"I just want to know cuz I worry about you."

Showing Zaria his left and right fist's, with a grin, James said, "don't worry, I can take care of myself, because I have this, and this."

"It's not funny when you have a golf ball on your head."

"Nah, I'm jokin; it was a fight and I got hit, that's usually what happens when you get in a fight, right? "

"To other people, not you."

"I can say this, I didn't plan it, and I don't plan on going to any more parties at places I don't know about, how's that?"

"Whatever, just stop fighting." They sat and talked until it was time for James to leave. Zaria reminded him she couldn't drop him off because her mom was using the car to go out with some of her friends. James jokingly responded, "I ain't worried, my feet work."

"Ha, ha, ha, ha really funny." When James got home, he sat with his brother watching T.V. while his dad cooked dinner. "Alright fella's, let's eat." Andrew blessed the the table with the Lord's Prayer, they ate and discussed the day's events - but James didn't tell his dad about his new allegiance with the vice lord's; he'd keep that to himself, and outside of the house. James discussed Jihad with his dad because he wanted to know what he thought about it. His dad leaned back in in the chair and said, " whelp, in the book I gave you, Kly gives a general description or understanding of Jihad; it's pretty much the Arab-Quranic version. You must remember, man is his own worst enemy; therefore, the struggle or Jihad starts within. It's not as simple as an external fight, it's an internal fight as well. We have to struggle against the temptations within us that want to do wrong; that's the alternate definition of Jihad, and that's the one I focus on, and you should focus on too. In the future, when you read more, I will show you how to trace a lot of the religious concepts to the originators of those writings. Right now, just keep reading and asking questions.

Later in the week, while James was getting dressed, he heard a knock at his bedroom door.

"Yeah?"

"It's me." said his mom. "Come run some errands with me before you leave."

"Alright."

A few minutes later, they sat in the car with James asking where they were going.

Looking at him with the look only a mother could give, Pat said, "why you in a rush?"

"Nah, I was just wondering, that's all." The first stop was the grocery store, they picked up some greens and okra because James Sr. planned on making one of his famous meals, he called soulé de light; James thought it must be a version of his soul food French versions of whatever he was putting together.

They grabbed a few more items and left. As they entered the McDonald's parking lot, James thought his mom was treating him to a Big Mac or something, until he heard his mom ask the cashier, " Hi, can I get a job application please?" Ahhh, this is what she was up to, James thought.

They sat down at a table, and James filled out the application and gave it back to the cashier. On the way out. James asked his mom if she was going to buy him a burger, Facetiously responding she said, "Your dad is cooking his version of McDonalds at home."

James couldn't help but laugh, it was funny, but most importantly, it reminded him of his dad; he must be rubbin off on her James thought on the ride home. James also thought, it would be really funny had his mom known that that was the same McDonalds he hid in after a high-speed chase with the police. At that moment, he was also glad he didn't get caught. After they put up the groceries, and set up the kitchen so his dad could begin cooking when he got home, James headed to Zaria's.

He and Zaria drove to Circus Circus. It was nice and far from everyone. They played video games, shot pool, and ate a couple slices of pizza. It was somewhat their usual meeting. Her dad took the day off so her bedroom wasn't an option, and his was definitely not an option, so they opted to hang out and have a different kind of fun. While sitting and talking, James asked, "what kinda food your people cook?"

"I don't know, regular food, I guess."

"I mean soul food, Chinese food, stuff like that."

"Uh, whatever my mom cooks, it's nothing special."

"Maan, you have to try my dad's cooking, he's absolutely the best, he can cook all kind of stuff, and he makes stuff up to cook." James told Zaria to hold up as he headed for the phone hanging on the wall. He returned and told Zaria she was invited to dinner.

"O.k., I'll let my parents know. And she headed for the phone to call and let her parents know she was going to James' house for dinner. On the drive to James' house, Zaria thought, I hope they like me, I wonder if my hair is ok., James interrupted her thought by asking her about her parents. " My parents are the same way; my mom took me to fill out a job application today, so I might have a job this summer. "Oh, that's cool, I know I'll have to get one sooner or later, especially when I get to college."

"What college you goin to?"

"I don't know yet, I want to stay in Minnesota because its closer. What about you?"

"I haven't really thought about it yet, since I have a few years of high school left. I'll give it some thought before I graduate; I'm sure my dad will have something lined up for me." They continued talking about college choices and graduation until they arrived at James' house. They sat on the couch talking with James' mom until they heard the famous " come an get it! " echoing from the kitchen. They sat, ate, and talked about James' and Zaria's trip to Circus Circus. James Sr. asked Zaria, " What do you think about my cooking?" Pointing at the greens with her fork, "this is really good."

"Oooh, you like the greens, well I have to confess, I make the best greens this side of the Mississippi."

Zaria with a mouth full of greens, smiled and responded, " Mmm Hmm."

James Sr. asked, "Where are your parents from?"

"My mom is America, and my dad is from India."

"Ahhh, o.k., so you might have some thugians in your blood line."

With a curious look on her face Zaria asked, "What's that?"

"Well, the thugians were like Robin Hood; they stole from the oppressor and gave to the oppressed. They have a great and long history amongst your people, you should do some research on them."

With a mouth full of greens she responded, "Mmm Hmmm." They finished the meal; James and Zaria sat on the couch talking until it was time for bible study. James walked her to the car, snuck in a kiss, made plans to meet tomorrow, and headed into the house.

Later that week, James heard the phone ring while he was reading, he hurried to the phone because he thought it was Zaria until he heard: " is Mr. James Blakely in?"

"Yeah, this is he."

"Hi, My name is Jane, and I'm calling about the application you filled out."

"Oh yeah, what's up?"

"I'm calling to schedule an interview, when will you be available?"

"Uhh, whenever you want to."

"O.k., how's Thursday at one p.m.?"

"I'll be there." said James, as he wrote down the appointment on the note pad next to the phone. James hung up the phone with excitement, wondering what it would be like to have a job. James headed up stairs to finish reading. That evening, he told his parents about the interview as they ate dinner. His dad responded, " R.E.S.P.E.C.T; that's what Aretha Franklin said, I say, R.E.S.P.O.N.S.I.B.I.L.I.T.Y, that's what a J.O.B, will give you." His dad sounds like Big Bird with all the spelling, thought James as he rolled his eyes and looked at the ceiling.

That Thursday, James woke up and did the usual until he left for his interview. He was sure to be on time because he checked the bus schedule. On the way to the interview he wondered what sort of questions he would have to answer. He arrived at his stop, and went into the McDonald's. For some reason, every time he entered the restaurant, he could only remember being chased by the police.

The interview took about an half hour; the manager verified a few things on the application, and gave him another date to show up for training. Instead of going home, he headed to Joe's house to see what they were up to. He hung out at Joe's until they went to play basketball, James didn't play because he had his interview clothes on, so he watched everyone else play.

After the game, as they were leaving, James was talking to Reggie when he heard Joe say: " fuck you bitch." As he turned to see who Joe was talking to, Joe punched some guy they were playing basketball with. James saw another person approaching Joe from behind. James immediately ran over and punched him in the side of his head as hard as he could, while James and the other guy were fighting, Someone grabbed James from behind and threw him to the ground, as he began wrestling to try to get the person of him; Reggie kicked the guy in the face and yelled, "let him go bitch." James got up and noticed it was another me-lee he had gotten into. The fight lasted until they heard the gym coordinator say he was calling the police. That's when everyone ran in different directions. James left with Joe while everyone else left with Reggie to go to Chelle's house.

As they arrived at Joe's house, James felt his eye was swollen. He asked Sammy what his eye looked like; "it's a little swollen bruh, it's cool though."

Asking Joe, James said, "what the hell was that about?"

"That's the dude, the one that's always foulin' me. I told him, I was gonna beat his ass."

"Who is he? Where does he live?" asked James.

"That's the punk that be with Will an nem, he ain't shit though." James leaned back on the couch and thought, whelp, he might not be, but his boy got me good with a punch to the eye. Joe said, "fuck em' bruh, we'll see his ass again. Dude's a bitch, he always gets tough when he's with his boys." James sighed loudly and said, "I gotta get home and put some ice on my face."

On the way home James didn't think about the fight much, he wanted to get some ice before his eye was swollen shut. While he was placing ice in a towel his dad was coming from his office to the kitchen. He saw James with the ice on his face, and said, "What happened to you?"

"I got into a fight at the park." James gave him the particulars of the fight as he held the ice on his eye.

"Is it over?"

"Yeah, I think so, it was just a fight over a foul."

"Well, make sure you be careful and protect yourself, and don't provoke a fight; always take the peaceful approach." James Sr. said, as he walked up stairs to his bedroom.

James sat there nursing his eye for a while, then headed up the stairs, changed clothes, took a shower, and went to bed with a towel full of ice on his face.

That Friday, James headed to Vino's after he left Zaria's to attend a goal. When he arrived, it was the usual crew plus a few other people he didn't know, but was introduced to. Before the goal was opened, Vino pulled James to the side to speak with him. "I heard about the incident at the park."

"Uh uh," James responded with a nod. "That's good that you aided that brotha Joe, but, you have to get to him before he gets started - remember, our first approach is peace because we never want unnecessary conflict, we're always in a position of protecting ourselves."

James nodded in agreement with Vino and said, " o.k."

"Let's open this thing. Alright ya'll, lets get started."

Fred opened the goal. June was a brotha James met that day, he'd been outta town, so James wasn't introduced to him. He seemed pretty cool, he was an older brotha with a bulky frame, he had eyes that seemed to look through a person, and when he spoke it was through clenched teeth because he kept a toothpick in his mouth. They stood in a circle with their palms raised in front of them as June recited - " In the name of Allah, most gracious most merciful. Praise be to Allah, the cherisher and sustainer of the worlds; most gracious most merciful, master of the day of judgement. Thee do we worship, and thine aid we seek. Show us the straight way, the way of those on whom thou has bestowed thy grace, those whose portion is not wrath, and who go not astray." After the opening, a tall stocky brotha with a bald head and goatee named Cedric asked if there were any issues that had to be addressed before they moved on to business.

The goal lasted almost two hours, as they discussed upcoming events, the meaning of the literature that was passed out to be remembered the following week; the incident at the park, and how to handle situations like that peacefully. After the meeting, they stood in the circle with their palms raised as Cedric recited the holy divine to close the goal. Later, as James sat talking to Fred, Vino pulled him aside and told him to remember the stuff on the sheet he gave him so he could recite it in the future.

James shook hands, and said his goodbyes to everyone because he made arrangements to go back to Zaria's before he headed home. That night he relaxed on his bed and began looking over the paper Vino gave him. He took note of the prayer used to open the goal titled, the Al-Fatihah, and the one used to close the goal titled, the Holy Divine. He made note that both pieces of literature made mention of Allah. Hmmm; I wonder if this is something from the Nation of Islam, he thought. Never-the-less, he kept reading to get an idea of what he had to remember. After giving the papers a once-over, he placed them in his backpack hanging in his closet for safe keeping. The next day, he and Zaria went to Circus Circus, this time James brought Andrew along because he was always in the house, and his friends in the neighborhood were either in a summer camp, or doing something with their family. They played video games and ate cheese fries until it was time to go. That night at dinner, Zaria ate at James' house and went home. Later that evening Andrew asked his brother when they were going to Circus Circus again. James smiled and responded, "Never."

"Coooome ooooon,"

"You're not fly enough to hang with me." Andrew threw a light punch at James, " you're not fly enough to be with me."

"Nah, I don't know, I have a job now so I have to figure out my schedule because I'm a Big dog."

The next day while watchin T.V. James was interrupted.

"James, telephone." said Andrew.

"Hello, said James as he put the phone to his ear.

"Hi, this Jane at McDonalds, I'll be holding a training session Friday and I need you to be there at one o'clock."

"O.k., I'll be there."

As he hung up, he said, "yeeeah boooy" to his brother as he grabbed Andrew and playfully put him in a headlock. "I am a working man, so you peasants be gone."

"You goofy, that's what you is."

"Ahhhh, how dare you talk to Hulk Hogan like that ,little peasant?" said James as he grabbed Andrew and placed him in a headlock, James and Andrew wrestled in the living room a little while before James made him submit, so he could get back to remembering the holy divine.

Since James had to work Friday, his recitation would have to wait until a later date. Vino told him when James called to notify him of his work schedule that he could recite the literature whenever he had a Friday off. James first day of orientation was o.k., he thought. He sat and watched a cleanliness and safety video; he received a uniform, that, to his surprise, fit nice. The Monday, Wednesday, and Saturday afternoon schedule was alright with James. Since the job was part time until he went back to school that fall, he'd make a little money and eat some free Micky D's. Who'd pass that up? He pondered. After orientation, he headed home to wash his uniform and go see what Zaria was up to. After he arrived at Zaria's they continued where they'd left off in her bedroom. James laid back after they explored each other's passions and he started thinking about how good it felt to be here with Zaria; he hoped it would never end, while he stared at her sleeping.

That evening was the usual at his house. He talked, joked, and laughed with his dad, brother, and mom while they talked about his first job; his dad called it a gig. James Sr. always had some foreign word that he'd use and it would take James forever to figure it out, because his dad wouldn't tell him what it meant. After bible study James headed up stairs to get some rest because he had to work tomorrow.

"Oh, o.k.," James said as he was shown how to turn off the buzzer that let him know when the fries were done. "When do I get to move up to the register?" James asked Ron, his medium height chubby co-worker that wore a short afro, that was flat in the back.

"Ahhh, it'll be a while because they want you to learn fries, then burgers, so don't hold your breath."

"How long you been working here?"

"A couple years, it's cool, I have a decent shift so I can't complain."

"My shifts are cool too."

"You're part time, so you'll be in and out of here before you know it."

"Whatever the time, I'll be alright with it." Ron and James talked for a moment while James tended to the fries, and Ron went back and forth from the drive thru. After James' shift, he went home and slept until dinner. He figured he was tired because he was on his feet for a few hours, and doing all sorts of stuff his manager Jane would have him doing. Damn, I didn't think that would make me tired, thought James.

That night, he barely heard his dad talk at bible study; his mind was preoccupied with getting some sleep. After bible study, James headed up stairs and slept until the next morning.

"Zaria's on the phone," said Andrew as he woke James.

"Alright." He picked up the receiver and told Zaria to come over because he was too tired to walk to her house. Half-hour later, Zaria arrived to find James sleeping on the couch.

"Why are you so tired?"

"I went to work yesterday for like five hours, and the job zapped all my energy."

"Whelp, get up sleepy head, and let's go somewhere."

"Nah, I'ma just lay here for the rest of the day; you can chill with me. My mom and dad won't say anything, as long as we're not doing anything nasty."

"Alright, what's on T.V.?".

"Nothin, you can figure it out, while I go back to sleep." Zaria watched T.V., and talked to Andrew while James slept. That evening Zaria stayed for dinner. James Sr. teased her and asked if she would like to be adopted.

Zaria laughed, and said, " Yep."

That week James didn't have to work because his training was over so he could go to a goal. At Vino's James was introduced to a brotha named Dominique, he was a little taller than James, he had a muscular build with short curly hair. James hadn't met Dominique because he spent his time training at K.O.'s boxing gym, since he had won the Golden Gloves boxing championship, he was in the gym a lot, and to make ends meet, he was a bouncer at Norma Gene's night club. That's cool, a vice lord that's a golden gloves champion at twenty-two years old, it can't get better than that.

"Alright ya'll let's open" said, Vino. They discussed the usual and congratulated Dominique on the championship, as they rounded off business, Vino said, "close it out James." Vino caught James by surprise, he didn't think he would have him close the goal, James sighed and said: "On this holy divine day, I give praise to Allah, father of the universe; on this holy divine day we give a special prayer for the brothers who have lost their lives for the upliftment and salvation of this nation. For it is forbidden to eat any animal that has been beaten, scald, or strangled to death. From my right hand is Allah, Father of the universe. From my left hand is Satan, Dragon, the beast; I close this demonstration with the five golden points of the star love, truth, peace, freedom, and justice."

As they gathered after the goal, Vino pulled James aside and congratulated him on remembering the lit so fast. He then gave him a few more sheets of literature. " I'm giving you these because if you memorized the little bit I gave you, I'm sure you can remember this. Remember, this stuff is to be acted out, not just recited. Adapt to it, because this is a way of life. You're a lot sharper than most of these other brotha's and sista's, so rely on the lit to operate and you won't go wrong."

"Alright, I'll memorize this and get back to you."

That night, James, C, Ray, Jason, Louie, and Chelle went to a party on 35th and 4th. James thought it was a waste of time because they could have their own gathering, why take a bus half way across town to hang out. Once they were at the party, James thought it was alright, though the fried chicken wings were good; the party wasn't what Jason thought it was going to be, James thought, this is wack. "Let's go," said James.

"Yeah, this is kinda slow," said Chelle. They left and headed for the bus stop. The bus schedule read that the bus wouldn't be there for another half hour. Since it was a cool summer night, they decided to hang at the bus stop and wait on the bus. As they sat there talking and joking, Jason noticed the same light brown ninety-eight Oldsmobile drive by. That was the second time he'd seen that car in the last four or five minutes. Jason warned them to look out for the car.

A few minutes had past, as Chelle looked to her left, she saw the car leap around the corner speeding towards them. The car came to a screeching halt in front of the bus stop, and the doors flew open, James looked and David said, " what's up now pussy?"

As James got into a fighting stance, he saw three other guys with David; he recognized G-Man and Bishop, the bald-head guy with a medium build and a gold tooth he didn't recognize, and he didn't have time to sit and play put the face on Mr. Potato head either. As they rushed the bus stop swingin. James punched David in his nose, David immediately bent over, grabbing his nose with blood rushing between his fingers. James grabbed him around the neck and waist of his pants, and slammed him into the bus stop shelter head first; James heard him moan as he laid on the ground. When he looked up, he saw Joe and Chelle fighting the guy with the gold tooth. As he was throwing punches at them with his back to the car, James ran over to help them; he quickly dove to the ground when he heard pop, pop, pop, pop. He thought he was being shot at, when he looked up, he saw Jason pointing a gun, and G-Man running across the street, while Bishop was lying on the side walk curled in the fetal position holding his stomach. Instantly, they ran.

CHAPTER SIX

JUSTICE

T hat was the first time James had seen someone get shot; the first incident with Joe wasn't anything compared to this, he thought as he laid across his bed the next day. Damn, dude was hurtin. T.V. is not even close to how dude was in pain. After work, James stopped at Joe's to hang out for a little while before he headed to Zaria's. As he sat on the couch in Joe's basement, Joe said, " that bitch told on Jason bruh."

"Who?"

"That bitch David and nem."

"What are you talkin about?"

"Maaan, Jason is in jail for poppin that mothafucka Bishop."

"How'd they know it was him, we didn't say nothin."

"That punk David or one of them bitches with him, snitched on Jason bruh. Can you believe that shit?"

"Damn, I hope they don't say anything about me."

"I'ma catch that donut as mothafucka and split his fuckin head like a cantaloupe." Leaning back into the couch staring at the ceiling James said, "Bruh, I hope they don't start pointin fingers at us."

"If they do, so what; that's just gonna make me kill they ass."

James shook his head in disbelief, this shit is gettin outta hand, I'll holla at Vino and ask him what I should do, thought James. James sat and listened to Joe yell about killin David and his friends for an hour, then decided he'd had enough and headed to Zaria's.

"Hey, what's up babe" said, Zaria.

"You know me, cool as a fan."

"Come on let's go talk,"

They entered her bedroom, Zaria lay across the bed and James gently lay on top of Zaria, kissed her, and proceeded to lick her neck. "Hol' up" Zaria said, as she removed her shirt and bra, and laid back on the bed. James lightly kissed his way down her caramel skin, taking his time, he licked Zaria's breast as she lightly moaned and gently rubbed the back of James' head. James continued down her body, unzipping her pants, gently pulling them off, he removed her white satin panties, and saw Zaria's dark V-shaped love triangle.

His heart raced as he removed his clothes. James continued to lick and kiss on Zaria's body until he gently penetrated her, as he slid inside Zaria, he could feel her wetness while she moaned; James continued listening to her moans for the next hour until his body shuttered and relaxed. Afterwards, they lay there with Zaria's back against his chest, like they were two spoons and slept. That night James called Vino. And told him about Jason being locked up over the incident at the bus stop. Vino told James they'd discuss it at his house, and to come over the next day.

"Come on in brotha," said, Vino.

James sat back on the couch and Vino said, " so what's the deal with Jason's situation?"

"Well, we were standing there minding our business and the folks rode down on us, and all hell broke loose. The next thing I know, Jason popped Bishop because they were tryin to jump him while we were fightin."

"O.k., I see. Well, let me tell you this. Always protect yourself against any force against you. Jason didn't do anything wrong; had they beat him to death, then what? What he did is called justice. Justice works in many ways, and that's one of them; do you understand that principle?"

"From what you're saying, yeah."

"That's why I gave you that other lit, Hol' up, I'll be right back." James sat there thinking about what Vino told him about justice, Vino interrupted his thought when he entered the living-room. "Listen to this, justice is the order that rules between ones higher self and lower self, it should always stand on truth. Here, we have a clear definition of justice. Jason was right in protecting himself; though we strive to deal with people using our higher selves, or the higher reasonable mind. Sometimes, we have to use the low and the sword of justice has to prevail."

"Yeah, I got it."

"Another thing you have to be careful of is them Roma soldiers; they'll lie and twist the truth, and convince you to tell on your own, don't fall for it. Always ask for a lawyer. James nodded in agreement; he spent the rest of the day at Vino's learning lit, and asking questions about books he'd read, and James learned that Vino had done time in Illinois.

That Thursday everyone decided to go to Powderhorn Park. James was against going because it was too far, and he didn't want to be on the bus or in a stolen car. Louie lived by Powderhorn.

"It ain't that far," said Joe.

"Nah, I'm cool, ya'll can go." said, James.

"Come on man, Shawn's gonna be up there hoopin," said, Joe. He ain't no hooper, thought James.

"We can get Steph to take us." said, Shawn.

"If we can get a ride there and back, I'll go", said James.

Joe went to the pay phone and called Steph to get the mini-van, meet them at the bowling alley, and take them to Powderhorn. As James sat in a chair watchin people bowl, he heard Joe say, "come on bruh, she's here." James turned and saw Steph was a short white girl with long brown hair, light blue eyes, and large breasts. As he approached her, Shawn introduced her to James; " this is one of the honorary sista's, Steph."

"Hi" she said in a high-pitched voice.

Putting his arm on James' shoulder, Shawn said,

"this is James, he's one of the illustrious brotha's from the South Side."

Steph smiled and said, " I see that."

"Let's go ya'll," said Joe.

"I got shotgun," said Shawn.

"Come on, let me get in the front." said Louie.

"Nah, my legs are longer than yours," said Shawn. As they got in the van, Steph drove them towards the park. When they turned on Lake Street, a police car got behind them and followed them for two blocks, then turned onto another street.

"Fuck them punks, they just tryin to scare somebody," said Ray.

"They probably ran Steph's plates and saw she was legit," said Louie.

In an excited voice, Ray said, "We legiiiit biiitch."

Steph parked in the parking lot, and they went inside to the gym. Jason, C, and Steph sat on the bleachers, while everyone else played ball. The game was going good until Ray made a basket and said, "ya'll nigga's can't play no ball, it's south-side nigga."

Someone yelled, "fuck the south-side nigga, it's north-side, it's north-side in here."

"Ya'll nigga's still can't hoop," said Ray.

A medium height dark-skinned guy that stood taller than Ray, walked over to him and said, " so whatchu sayin nigga?"

"Maaan, listen. I'm sayin fuck you nigga," said Ray. And followed his comment up with a punch to his chin. As the dark-skinned guy hit the floor, Ray kicked him between his legs, That's when the other guy's from the north-side rushed in Ray's direction. C told Steph to go start the van and wait on them, he then ran towards the fight. James did more wrestling than throwing punches, the guy he was fighting wouldn't let him go. Shawn had no problem throwin punches, his arm length ensured no one would grab him. As everyone fought in the gym, James heard the heavy set gym attendant say: " break it up, break it up, or I'm callin the police."

That was the cue for everyone to run out the front door, and jump into the van. As they rushed into the van, Steph asked, "are you guys o.k.?"

"Yeah, were cool, I can't say much for them other studs though," said Shawn.

As they drove off James thought, I'm glad it wasn't any shootin.

For the next month, James stayed away from basketball games, unless it was with his dad. He studied his lit, hung out with Zaria, attended goals, and studied with Vino. Vino took James under his wing because he saw James was sincere, and would be an elite member of the nation someday. He had never met anyone who could memorize, recite, and apply the lit as fast as James had. James continued this routine until school started.

Though it had been a few months since James was back at school, it was the usual day-to-day of hittin the books. The only difference was James' classes. He definitely got

a shop class, and the Driver's Ed class; the shop class would let him out of school half an hour early. The rest of his classes were cool, the way he saw it, it was just a bunch of reading and writing, no biggy. He'd ace whatever class he had.

At lunch, James and Joe headed to Burger King to get a bite to eat. As they were talking and walking James was startled when he heard the tires of a car screech, and a loud boom that followed. " It was only a car accident," said Joe.

"Man, I didn't know what that was, I had to jump."

"Ain't nothin to be scared of."

"The last time I heard tires screech like that, was that situation with Jason."

"Shit, I was there, I ain't trippin though."

"Bruh, to be aware is to be alive. I intent on livin for a while, so when I hear a strange noise, I'm lookin to see what it is." As they headed to Burger King, James thought about Jason. He received two years in a place called Red Wing for shootin Bishop. Damn, that's a long time, thought James as he bit into his hamburger; James sat wondering what Zaria's school schedule was like. He knew she had cheer leader practice, was he wouldn't see her as much - he'd figure something out, I think the weekends will be our time, thought James.

That Friday, James used Zaria's house as an excuse to go to the goal at Vino's. It was the usual goal, but everyone noticed how well James could recite the Al-Fatihah. He was so good, he recited in Arabic. James learned a lot about the Islam over the summer, it was something Vino taught him. After the goal, James headed to Zaria's to see what she was up to, and to make plans for Saturday night, Zaria had access to the car, so she'd pick him up at his house. That Saturday, Zaria picked James up and headed downtown to the Sky Way. They sat and watched the movie, as much as they could between kissing and fondling each other. After the movie, James and Zaria were headed across Hennepin Avenue when he heard someone knocking on a restaurant window next to the movie theatre, when James turned to look, he saw Cassandra, Chelle, and Vino. He and Zaria turned towards the restaurant. James hadn't noticed that this place sold pasta when he was down here before.

"What up, lil lord?" said Vino.

"What up bruh,"

"Heeey, what's goin on big bruh," said Chelle.

"What's up James?" said, Cassandra.

"I'm cool, what ya'll up to?"

Vino said, "I'm down here buyin them some clothes, "

James pulled Zaria close to him and said, "this is my girl Zaria." Waving, Zaria said, "hi."

"Come on, chill with for a while," said Vino. They sat down and talked about where they were going to go shopping, ate some pasta salad, and made their way up the street to the City Center so Chelle and Cassandra could get a few outfits. As they were walking up Hennepin Avenue, James noticed David, Robbie, and G-Man. James immediately turned towards Zaria and said, "go start the car."

Zaria could tell by the tone of his voice that he was serious; she immediately turned and went in the direction of the parking lot. As they approached the City Center entrance Chelle said to David: "Why you snitch on Jason?"

"I ain't snitch on nobody, bitch." Instantly, Vino punched David in the face and he hit the ground with a thud. Chelle and Cassandra rushed G-Man, and began slicing him with box cutter's they carried in their purses. James and Vino got hold of Robbie, threw him to the ground and hit him with a fury of blows that left him unconscious. As James got up to kick Robbie in the head, James heard a horn honk, he looked up, and saw Zaria had stopped the car in front of the City Center. They piled in the car and Zaria pulled off. Zaria drove through downtown like it was a maze she knew by heart, she pulled over several blocks away and asked where Vino parked, so she could take him to his car.

"Nah, let's get back over south, I'll get the car later." It was a silent ride to the south side, James thought, damn, Zaria was right on time. I thought we'd have to run to the car. Zaria pulled up at Vino's. Vino, Chelle and Cassandra got out, made plans to meet each other later and said their goodbye's. Zaria pulled off, asked James what he wanted to do; he told her to drop him off at his house, and he'd call her later to make plans to get together in the future. As Zaria pulled off, James thought, that mothafucka David; I'm goin to kill his ass.

The next day at lunch, James told Joe what occurred downtown, Joe responded, " ooooh, I wish I was there bruh."

"It was cool, we had it covered."

"Awww shit, chief knocked his ass out though?"

"Yeah, a straight up boon to the face, and he was outta there."

"That's that shit he learned in prison bruh. I heard he's a cold piece with his hands. Imagine if Dominique was there, oooo weeeee, it would've gotten ugly."

"Shit, Chelle and Cassandra wasn't no joke either, they sliced G-Man's ass up like a cake, pssss, it was a sad day for him."

"Well, they deserved that shit for snitchin on Jason anyway; fuck em bruh." As Joe talked about how he would've smashed David's face in after he hit the ground, James thought, that's justice served on a silver platter. That Friday at goal, it was tense because everyone knew about the fight downtown, and they were waitin to see if Vino would give the go ahead to demonstrate justice on sight, as Vino would've said. Instead, he said the particular ones don't know any better, and we should avoid them because anyone who doesn't mind gettin beat down every time they cross our paths is a damn fool. And damn fools will get you in a lot of trouble.

That weekend, James hung out with Zaria, avoiding any place he thought a damn fool would hang. For some reason, he couldn't get that damn fool David out of his mind. He couldn't figure out why this dude stayed on his mind- damn, he thought. On Monday, it was the usual school day, James left school early because he had shop class, so he decided to head home and do some homework to avoid doing it later.

James turned the corner and there stood David, with a large .38 revolver so big, it could hardly fit in his hand. The chrome was so bright, that it nearly blinded James. He heard David's sinister voice say, "coooome heeeere niiigaaa." As James turned and ran, it seemed like he couldn't get far enough away to avoid being shot. He heard endless shots being fired at him, the air smelled like gun smoke, as he saw his dad running toward him, James heard, pop, pop, pop, pop, pop, pop, pop. James felt each bullet hit him, but he couldn't fall until he reached his dad's outstretched arms. He was saying something, but James couldn't make it out because David's voice overshadowed his dad' voice - how could this be.

"James, James, get up," said Andrew as he shook James out of his sleep. James laid there staring at Andrew as if he didn't know him. He could feel each spot on his body tingling from the bullets that hit him in his dream.

"Zaria's on the phone." James came to his senses, and realized he was dreaming, phew, I thought I was a goner, he pondered as he headed down stairs to talk to Zaria. The next day at the bus stop, James, Joe, and Sammy were standing there waitin on the bus when Joe asked him if he'd heard about Chelle. "Nah, what's up with her?"

"Some girls jumped her at school the other day."

"For real?"

"Yeah, some G.D. hoe's that go to her school heard about that shit her and Cassandra did to G-Man. I guess he messes with one of them traps."

"How's Chelle doing?"

"She's cool, them ho's just scratched her face up, it ain't shit though."

"So what's up with Cassandra?"

"She wasn't there, but she'll be there this time."

"What time you talkin about?"

"The time when we finna go up to Roosevelt and get them ho's in order, Bruh, that's chief's lil cousin, ain't no body gettin away with that shit."

"I hear that, when Ya'll goin?"

"Today at lunch, Steph is gonna take off work and pick us up at Burger King."

"Like the song says: I'llll bee theeeeere."

James couldn't sit still in any of his classes. He kept focus and took notes, but the fact that he knew it was going to be a fight excited him, not because he liked fightin, he hoped David would be there so he could beat his ass. We'll be serving justice on a silver platter today, he thought.

That afternoon, they met at Burger King. James counted the usual people he's usually with, plus Cedric and Fred; Chelle and Cassandra were already in Steph's minivan. James jumped in the back seat of Fred's 1978 Buick Skylark as they headed to Roosevelt.

"Dig this, I'm gonna drop ya'll off a block away from the school, so our cars aren't seen by anyone. When ya'll get done taking care of business, run a block over from where I drop you off - o.k.?" said Fred.

When they were dropped off, they got out and walked to the school. They went to the side door by the cafeteria, and Chelle saw the three girls that jumped her and said, "There go them bitches." Chelle and Cassandra briskly walked up to the light-skinned girl without notification, and started punching her in the head and face. The other two girls jumped in, the heavy-set one punched Chelle in the side of the head, as Chelle staggered, Joe ran and drop kicked the girl from the side, and said, "Don't ever hit my people bitch." And proceeded to punch her in the face. The third girl decided it was in her best interest to run into the school. After Chelle recuperated from the punch to the side of her head, she grabbed the heavy set girl by the hair and used her free hand to place heavy blows to her face.

"Hey, hey, break it up," screamed a stocky black school security guard, as he grabbed Joe by the collar. That's when the security guard was bum-rushed by Steve, Reggie, Louie, and Rico. They threw kicks and punches to just about every part of his body. He tried his best to fight them off, but it was too many of them. James heard him say, "uuuh," as he hit the ground from a punch that landed square on his chin. "You fuckin bitch, don'tchu ever touch me, " yelled Joe.

"Come on ya'll let's go," said Ray. James had to grab Chelle because she was on top of the light-skinned girl who was in the fetal position covering her head tryin to cover up from the blows to her face and head.. They all ran in the direction the cars were parked. They arrived at the cars and jumped in. As the cars headed in the opposite direction of the school, they could hear sirens. Fred pulled over and waved to Steph to pull over.

"What's up," said Steph.

"Dig, everybody duck down and you drive at the speed limit."

"O.k.," said Steph as she drove off. Fred drove two blocks, turned into an alley, found an empty parking space behind someone's house, and parked. They sat there for an hour or so, then drove to Burger King to drop everyone off.

"Alright, ya'll be cool and I'll see ya'll later," said Fred as he backed out of the parking space at the restaurant. James didn't see Steph's minivan, they probably went to Chelle's house, he thought as he and Joe decided to walk to Joe's house.

"Damn bruh, I think I broke my hand on that bitches head."

"It'll be alright."

"She had a hard head bruh. Hey, did you see that swole ass mothafucka grab me? I couldn't get out that shit for nothin. If ya'll hadn't been there, I'd of been hurtin for certain."

"You'll be alright. Just get some ice on it when you get home. Let me see, it's o,k., it doesn't look broke. I thought ol' girl was gonna whoop yo ass."

"Shiiiiit, the day a bitch woops my ass is the day the earth stops spinnin. You see the other skeezer run? That shit was so funny; she looked like she could fight as ugly as she is. I guess I don't know much about women."

"Them girls didn't want no problems, when they saw Chelle, their eyes got big as hell. Chelle was on em' so fast they couldn't do nothin but pretend to fight back. They would've been better off runnin."

"Hey, I know them donut's are gonna be mad when they see what Chelle did to that girls face. Did you see all that blood? Damn, that was some nasty shit to see bruh." As they got to Joe's house James said, " alright, I'ma head home. I'll see you in the morning, make sure you put some ice on your hand - mighty."

Chapter Seven

Revenge is Best Served Cold

Whatchu been up to, I haven't seen you around the house much." Said James Sr.

"I'm here every day." Said James.

"Yeah, at bible study, and at our basketball games. That girl Zaria gotchu hooked huh?"

"Nah, we just kick it when we can because her schedule is busy."

"So, where you been?"

"At Chelle's house."

"Chelle. Ahhh, you got some playa in ya blood, huh?"

"Nah, she's my homie, it ain't like that."

"That's what I used to say."

"You sound like Uncle Kenny."

"Nope. Uncle Kenny sounds like me. I'm the best that ever did it – I met your mom and she got me hooked, and my player days were over. It'll happen to you sooner or later. Alright, let me leave you to your homework."

That night after bible study, James talked to Zaria for a few hours, and made plans to see her Friday, Saturday, and Sunday. That week was the usual day-to-day activities.

James enjoyed his shop class because he got out of school early, and he learned how to use a lathe. He talked with his dad about the Driver's Ed class, because he wanted to teach him how to drive. On Saturday, James and Zaria went to Minnehaha Falls to enjoy the weather and watch the falls before it got too cold. The frigid winters in Minnesota were treacherous. Though it snowed in Gary, it seemed colder in Minnesota. They talked about school, family, and friends. Zaria was persistent in knowing about James' friend's, especially the two females, Chelle and Cassandra. James' response to her inquiry was honest, but Zaria seemed suspicious. "We're just like brothers and sisters."

"I don't see too many brothers and sisters sit on each other's laps."

Grabbing his head in disbelief, "We were in the car speeding through downtown tryin not to get caught by the police. We were in a rush."

"Well, you could've gotten in the front seat."

"Did you see what happened? If we stood there tryin to figure out who would sit where, we'd probably be in jail right now."

"So, how long have you known them?"

"A little while."

"What's a little while?"

"Look, first of all. Chelle is messin with Ray, and she's Vino's cousin; that's one reason why I wouldn't mess with her. You need to stop trippin."

"I ain't trippin. What about the other girl?"

"Who, Cassandra? Maaan, Cassandra is cool with me too, but it's not like that, F.R.I.E.N.D.S., that's all, calm down."

They talked about James' female friends for a few minutes, until James told her he had to get home because he's supposed to be at Joe's. Zaria sarcastically asked if his other friends were going to be there. James shook his head and headed toward the car so she could take him home. Though the radio was on, the drive was silent, James couldn't believe she thought he was messin around with other girls. He hoped that she would believe him because he couldn't keep going through the jealousy fits. When they arrived at James' house, Zaria told him to call her that night. He acknowledged her request and headed into the house. He never made it to Joe's, he used that as an excuse to get away from the argument. He hated arguing because it made him mad, and lately, with all the stuff goin on, he seemed more edgy and ready to fight; at certain times, willing to kill. He went to him room, laid back on the bed thinkin about the last situation at the school. James laughed to himself, thinkin; justice served cold by the sista's. He laid there thinkin where that situation would go when David and his boy's heard about it. With G-Man's face sliced, Bishop getting shot, and those girls getting the beat down, James was sure there was going to be some revenge. He figured, keeping a close eye at school, he didn't doubt they would arrive at his school. This was Chelle's last year, it would be hard to find her alone after she graduated. Steph lived in Richfield, the possibility of them running across her was slim, she only came around she wasn't working or on the weekends. As for everyone else, the possibilities became slimmer as James went down the list. They usually were together ninety percent of the time, unless they were at home. He doubted anyone would show up at their houses. He thought about different ways anyone could get to him while he was alone, then the dream came to him, all he thought about was the .38.

Two weeks later at school, Joe told James to meet him at the gym because they all had to talk. That morning, James couldn't seem to stop thinkin about what Joe was up to. He hated when he wouldn't just say what was on his mind; that afternoon, James, C, Joe, Ray, Louie, Shawn, and Steve stood there waitin on Joe to tell them what was goin on.

"What's up?" said Ray.

Joe said, "them donuts caught Rico at some girl's house and jumped him. He's in the hospital."

"What happened?" asked C.

"I guess him and Kev went over to some girls' house, and Dwayne, E, Lenny, and Lil' G were in the apartment below. When they were leaving, they jumped him and hit him with a bat, and stabbed him up and shit."

"What happened to Kev?" asked Ray.

"Shit, he ran and left him. Fred lookin for his ass too."

"Damn, how he just leave him like that?" Asked Louie.

"Man, that mothafucka got a serious V comin for that shit bruh, for real." Said Ray.

"So, what's up?" said James.

"Man you know what's up. When we catch them, it's on." Said Reggie. "We're goin to the hospital tomorrow night to see Rico, get the full story, and see how he's doin."

"Where's he at?" asked Louie.

"He's at Abbott." Said Joe.

"We'll meet at Vino's and go together tomorrow night." Said Ray.

That night, after James talked to Zaria, he thought about Rico's situation. This is something else, just when everything was cool, this pop's up. We gotta put an end to this stuff, I'm tired of looking over my shoulder every time I hear a tire screech, a loud noise. I wonder if we have Vino go to them and squash it, maybe that would work. They're so dumb, they might try to jump him for bragging points. I'll see what happens tomorrow. The next day, everyone met at Vino's, got in the cars, and headed to the hospital. James didn't like the smell of the hospital, it smelled stale and it was cold. When he saw Rico his heart seemed to skip a beat. Rico's head was swollen twice its regular size, his lips were swollen, his eyes were swollen, and the other was swollen shut. He had stitches in his bottom lip, and his head had a large piece of gauze in the spot where he was hit.

"What up bruh" said Vino.

"I'm cool, what's up with ya'll?" responded Rico.

"What up pretty boy?" said Shawn.

"I still got my hoe's. They ain't stop nothin. They had to cut my hair so they could put staples in my head."

"Don't worry bruh, get some rest, we gone handle this." Said Joe. Vino raised his hand at Joe to stop him room talking about revenge and said," We'll discuss that somewhere else."

Chelle held Rico's hand, and sat on the edge of the bed next to him. "I know you're a little hurt right now, but tell us what happened." Said Fred.

"Man, bruh, they came out of nowhere. We were upstairs at Co Co's, I guess they were in the bottom duplex. When we were leavin, they were on the front porch. So, me and Kev kept walkin, hopin they wouldn't notice us, that's when they came outside and started shit. I turned around, the next thing I know I was swingin."

"What was Kev doin?" asked Ray.

"Man, I don't know. I thought he was fightin. I couldn't see. After I was hit in the head, I tried to grab one of them so I wouldn't fall."

Vino sighed and said: "Damn, bruh, I'm sorry this happened. We can't relive the past, so we'll focus on the future. You'll be o.k., as long as you're alive, we'll move past this situation and be aware of our surroundings."

"Where were you at?" asked Ray.

"We were up on Grand by White Castle. It was a brown and white duplex on the corner. You remember when we got into it with them stud's at the house party over there, it was the first duplex on that block."

"Oh yeah, I remember it."

"That bitch didn't set you up did she?" asked Joe.

"Nah, I don't think she knew we were into with them cats. I met her at the City Center with her cousin."

They sat at a hospital for awhile, and tried to make Rico as comfortable as possible until the nurse told them visiting hours were over. On the drive to Joe's, Joe asked Vino: "What's up?"

"Anything can be up bruh; why, whatchu want to be up?"

"The same thing they want to be up, that shit can't fly, that could've been anyone of us."

"Sometimes patience is the best move."

"We've been too patient."

"So you think they're out runnin around partyin about what they did?"

"They might be."

"Human logic dictates, they know what they did was severe. Believe me when I tell you they're layin low."

"I hope so."

"Just be patient lil bruh, because revenge is best served cold."

They arrived at Joe's and got out. James decided to sit at Joe's for a little while and talk to him. "What's up?" said Joe.

James leaned back into the couch. "Man, this shit has to be taken care of ASAP."

"But, Vino said wait."

"Nah, he said be patient."

"So, whatchu wanna do?"

"If we had some guns, we can take care of business ourselves."

"Straight up? I'm wit it bruh."

"Listen, we can't say anything. It has to be us and no one else."

"We need a car to drive down there, it can't be anybody's care we know."

"I can get a car, don't worry about that. And, I can get the straps too."

"We'll meet next week and go over there when it gets dark and see what's up."

After they made plans, James went home before it got too late. His dad thought he was at Zaria's, so he'd be o.k.. On the way home, James had an urge to turn around an tell Joe he wanted to go up there that night. He thought against it, like Vino, he knew they were layin low; in the future, they'd be ready to venture out to get pats on the back from their cruddy friends. James thought Pops Arcade would be a better place to catch them, but there were too many witnesses. And they'd surely be in jail or worse. That night, James went to bed plottin on how to serve the revenge in his mind, as cold as possible.

Three days later, Joe told James to meet him at his house after school. James couldn't be there because it would be too late, and his dad would trip if he missed bible study. They made plans to meet that afternoon, James had shop class and would be leavin early – Joe would skip. They both left school and went to Joe's house. Joe's parents were at work, so the coast was clear. James sat on the couch in Joe's basement, Joe unwrapped a towel, and showed James two guns. One was a snub nose .38 revolver; the other was a semi-automatic hair trigger .9mm clock. James grabbed the .38, wrapped his hand around the butt of the gun as if he were squeezing a baseball; the feel of the gun in his hand was exhilarating. He pointed it at the basement wall, pretending to fire shots.

"This is it bruh." Said Joe.

Staring down the barrel of the gun, James said, "yeah, I like this."

"That's the trey-eight, it has six shots; this is the nine, it has sixteen shots. I have some extra clips for this, and some more bullets for yours too. Oh yeah, I got some black clothes, masks, and gloves too; we don't want nobody to see us. You got some black clothes you can wear?"

"Yeah, I got some black stuff. What's up with the car?"

"We'll get it the night we leave, I can't leave a stolen car sittin around, the police might find it."

"O.k., we're ready then. Remember, don't tell nobody about this, not even Vino."

"Alright bruh, I gotchu."

James and Joe sat at his house for a couple hours, until James decided to head home and do his homework.

The next few days were nerve wrecking, James couldn't get using the .38 out of his mind. He couldn't wait until he met David face-to-face with the .38. Somehow, he knew what David would feel like because of the bullets that hit him in his dream. He wondered if that's what it felt like to be shot.

"Hey, what's up James?" asked his mom, while she was stirring the gumbo she was preparing for dinner.

"Ah, nothin, just chillin." He sat down at the kitchen table. "Ma, have you ever had a scary dream?"

"Yeah, plenty of times, why?"

"Do dreams come true?"

"It depends on what kind dream you're talkin about."

"You know, the ones you have when you're sleepin."

"My grandmother used to tell me that dreams are a gateway to the future. If you paid attention to them, you could figure out what would happen in the future."

"Is that true?"

"I don't know. Why, you havin nightmares?"
"I was wonderin if the stuff you felt in dreams, you could feel in real life."

"What do you mean?"

"Like, if you get punched in a dream, does that punch feel the exact same in real life?"

"I don't know, that's a good question."

James sat and talked to his mom while she cooked – they talked about dreams, and how his relationship with Zaria was going. She laughed when James told her about Chelle and Cassandra being his other girlfriends in Zaria's mind. She told him, just don't let her see them so close. The next time, keeps his distance, and stop huggin all over other girls. They laughed about it, and talked about how she and his dad met after he got out of prison. James was surprised to know his dad was prison, he had never mentioned it. His mom told him, it's a part of his life he never talks about. She told him his dad had plenty of ladies around, and she fought a few times whenever they came around. When James was born, they got married, moved to Chicago until he was four, moved back to Gary when he was five, and have been together ever since. James thought that was cool, but his mind was still on his dad being in prison. They talked until his dad and Andrew came home. It was the usual night, with the exception that he wondered why his dad went to prison. James made sure not to ask because; he didn't want to upset him. So he decided it would be he and his mom's secret. Saturday couldn't come fast enough after James played basketball at the Y with his dad, he got permission to go to Zaria's. Instead, he went to Joe's; they dressed in black clothing and tucked their guns in the waists of their pants, and walked the few blocks to the bowling alley – "watch out for me." Said Joe.

James stood in the shadows of the building looking for anyone that might see Joe stealing a car. James heard the car engine come alive, then Joe drove in his direction. James hopped in the front seat. "Alrighty, let's go. Remember, if 5-0 gets behind us, get out and run."

"I didn't forget from the last time." They drove down towards Grand to see if they could catch David or anyone from his crew. Joe parked the car a block away from the brown and white duplex; he left the heat on because it was a cool fall evening. They sat there for a few hours and didn't see anyone, it seemed like the entire area was deserted. James leaned back in the car seat gripping the .38 thinking he couldn't wait to see David.

After another hour, Joe headed towards his house. As they drove, a police car turned in front of them. They couldn't believe they were following a police car in a stolen car with guns; both their hearts were beating faster than normal. James thought he could hear his heart beat. They followed the police car for two blocks, turned left on a side street, and took another route to Joe's house. They were both thinking, oooh shit.

The following week, James kept busy hangin out with Zaria a lot more, because he wanted to show her that she was the only girl he wanted to be with. His routine at home was the same, a lot of questions for his parents, and roughin up his little brother. That Friday, at the goal, James was shocked to see Kev. Damn, he thought, he's actually showin his face after what happened to Rico. After they conducted the usual opening and addressing other miscellaneous issues. The focus was on Kev. "Kev, stand in the middle of the circle, and explain to us what occurred with you, Rico, and them particular one's." said Fred.

"Well, we left Co Co's house and Rico squared up with one of them and another one stolen on him. That's when I started fightin some other dude who came out of the house. Once they started to jump me, I told Rico to come on, but he didn't want to run, so I ran."

"Well, brotha, you know you violated one of the eight principles. You are to aid and assist your brotha's at all times. You were supposed to go get that brotha, and make him run with you. Do you understand that?"

He stood shakin his head in agreement. "In the future, everybody in here has to be aware of what's goin on. If at any time your outnumbered, leave together. Alright, you got five minutes for not aidin that brotha." Kev stood in the middle of the circle, and three brotha's surrounded him. One read that Statement of Love to him, and they proceeded to violate Kev. They threw punches to the body, the chest – the face and groin area were off limits. Kev took so many hard blows, that he fell to the floor and covered his head; the violation went on for five minutes, after, he apologized and hugged all the brotha's at the goal.

Later that night, while Kev was sittin on the couch, James asked him if he was o.k.. Kev told him he was cool. And that he felt bad about the situation with Rico, he told Rico to come on, but he was tryin to fight all them dudes.

"Next time bruh, just be aware so all this mess won't happen again. I'll talk to Vino and have him holla at Rico about tryin to be Kung Fu."

"Alright bruh, thanks."

That Saturday, Joe and James parked in the same spot, so they could see anyone coming or going from the duplex. In an excited tone, Joe said, "There he is bruh."

"Who?"

"David's punk ass."

"Come on, let's go."

James slid on his mask, put on his gloves, and slipped out into the cool autumn night. They walked through a yard, so they could approach the duplex from the back. As they maneuvered their way up the alley hiding in the shadows of the garages, James and Joe slowly moved to the front of the house> When James crept around the corner he could hear David laughin; at the moment he felt the tension, as he crept around the corner, David turned, and his eyes got wide when he saw James stooped down dressed all in black holding a gun, David turned to run while yelling to everyone else that someone was ambushing them. Immediately, James opened fire, and David disappeared onto the enclosed porch. James and Joe ran up to the house and started firing into the porch. As they fled, James jumped over a person lying in the yard, and they disappeared into the night.

Three hours later, homicide detective Jones exited his car, walked up the sidewalk, and asked a police officer where the body was. He saw the usual; lights from police cars, yellow tape, the ambulance, in this case more than one, people crying, and spectators being nosy. He hated crime scenes like this because evidence always got messed up with people runnin around touchin the body, or the police not securing the crime scene in time.

"What we got here Mark?" asked Detective Roberts.

"Whelp, from what I see here, looks like a straight shot through the face." Said Mark.

"I heard the other victims were taken to the hospital, let me see. Oh, one is in critical, and two non-critical."

"This must've been serious because it looks like he was dropped here, and they continued in the direction of the house, and let off shots into the porch."

"What caliber?"

"I can't tell, we'll have to let forensics check it out."

"Well, whatever happened here was serious business, and whoever did this cold blooded."

CHAPTER EIGHT

THE LORD IS MY SHEPPARD

The next week, Detective Roberts looked into the victim's records to see who he was. After he placed his name in the computer, it read Damian Jones, 21 years old, from Chicago, Illinois. Roberts studied the face of the mug shot. Damian was dark-skinned, 5 feet 6 inches tall, about 170 pounds, with a bald head, the scars and tattoos showed he had a gold tooth, and several scars on his back and left arm. Roberts also took note, that he was a gangster disciple. The case smelled like gang warfare to Roberts. He was willing to bet the other victims were in the same gang.

"Got it."

"What's that?"

"The forensics report."

"What's it say?"

"You want to read it?"

"Nah, I trust you."

"Whelp, we have a .38 caliber that killed the victim. The .9mm was pulled out of one victim, and another .38 caliber was pulled from the neck of the one in critical."

"So we have two shoots, or we're looking for an octopus."

"Yeah, they also pulled some .9mms from the inside porch, and a few that went into the house. Boy, these guys were serious business, weren't they?"

"Well, our victim is Damian Roberts from Chicago, and he's affiliated with the gangster disciples."

"I guess we have a gang shooting then."

"Looks like it."

"The only thing we don't know is, what other gang did they have an issue with?"

"There's only one way to find out."

As detective Jones and Roberts walked between the automatic sliding doors of the hospital, detective Jones said, "Hey, Teressa, I'm looking for a Chris Crumwell, he was one of the victims in that eruption a few weeks back."

"Uhhh, he's in room 228."

"Thanks, you're a sweet heart."

"You promise?"

"Always."

Detective Jones and Roberts entered the hospital room and saw Chris with his leg in a sling, elevated in the air, and his neck was in a thick plastic brace pushing his neck in a position that had to be uncomfortable> Detective Jones said, "Heeey, Chris, What's happenin G?"

In a groggy and raspy voice, Chris said "I'm cool, what's up with you?"

With a sarcastic smile on his face, Jones said "I'm detective Jones, and that's my partna' Detective Roberts. We're here to let you know ya boy's a goner, and we need to know who gave him a .38 slug for his birthday."

Chris stared at them for a second trying to understand what he was saying and said, "Whatchu talkin about?"

"You didn't hear? Damian's dead."

He laid there with a blank star on his face, processing what he had heard. Detective Jones interrupted his thought saying, "Well, since you don't have anything to say, maybe you can tell us who you've been having an issue with, and we'll leave you to mourn."

With tears welling up in his eyes. Chris said, I don't know "whatchu talkin about."

"Suure you do. In fact, you were there when Mr. Robinson got shot, oh you don't remember who Bishop is? We did some digging around and found out: you, Damian, and Bruce were there. Bruce being Bishop."

"I don't know what you're talking about."

"Do you know that we; him and I, investigate attempted murder case? Yeah, we had Jason Edwards sent up shit creek without a paddle; yep, that's us."

"O.k., listen," said Detective Roberts. "You're not in any trouble, just tell us who did the shooting so we can get him off the streets. We're trying to help you. I know it was terrible to lose Damian, but we can solve it so you don't have to worry about being in the same box Damian's in."

"I don't know, they had on masks, that's all I know. I wasn't tryin to stick around and see who's shootin at me – I don't know."

"Here's my card, if you have any information, contact me, o.k.?"

"Alright."

As Detective Roberts and Jones sat in the car. Roberts offered Jones some coffee.

"Never touch the stuff."

"Come on, coffee is part of the daily diet."

"Nah, I'm a tea man."

"What are you, from England?"

"Ha, that's funny."

"Hey, how'd you do it?"

"Do what?"

"Get him to tell you who shot him."

"If you think someone's gonna put your head on a choppin block, what would you do?"

"I guess you're right."

"So, what's your next move?"

"The way I see it, the fruit never falls far from the tree; we look for Mr. Edwards friends."

"Bruce told us he didn't know the people, he only got out to fight because David Moore told him to."

"It seems to me, if Edwards is a Vice lord, just maybe, the people with him were too. Let's go visit some Vice lords."

The next few weeks, Detective Jones and Roberts spent time searching for people whose MO fit the crime. It wasn't until they got a hit on Vincent Blackwell that a light bulb went off in Jones' head. As Jones read his jacket, he wondered why he wasn't in prison. This guy is amazing thought Jones> Robberies, assaults, attempted murder, and an acquittal on a murder and under investigation fro two more in Illinois. Detective Jones pulled his prison record from Menard and Statesville in Illinois. Boy, this guy is serious. He's been through it all. Yeah his prints are definitely on this, Jones thought, as he reached for the phone to put an APB out on Mr. Blackwell. Almost a month later, Vino sat in the interrogation room staring at Detective Roberts. "Heeeellloooo Mr. Blackwell, I am your friendly neighborhood homicide detective here to pin a murder on you. Vino sat there staring at Detective Roberts. "You like to give the silent treatment huh. Well, I'll talk for you. You've done time in Statesville and Menard, and now you're going to do time in St. Cloud, Minnesota. Is that enough talking?"

Vino leaned back in the plastic chair and said "are you done playin games yet?"

"Oh, I assure you this is not a game. Look at this picture, you see that bullet hole in his head? Looks like some of your work in Chicago, doesn't it?"

"I wanna talk to my attorney. I don't have time to be playin with you Roman soldiers."

"Since you put it that way, before I mirandize you, let me say a prayer. I am not joking. I do this in all interrogations so people understand that the Lord will forgive their sins." Interrupted Detective Roberts. He lightly grabbed Vino's hand and recited the Lord's prayer. "there you have it, Mr. Blackwell. The Lord has forgiven your sins."

"Oh yeah?"

"Yeah Mr. Blackwell."

"That's funny, because my Lord is Allah, and he tells me not to talk to Roman soldiers – get me a lawyer or let me go."

"if that's what you want, we'll leave you to your thoughts about being charged with the murder of Damian Johnson. Have a good day sir, we'll be watchin you, so don't leave town." The detectives got up and left Vino sittin in the interrogation room, and went to their office. While Jones was leaning back in his black reclining chair, sippin a hot cup of tea, Roberts quizzed him about the Lord's prayer. And Jones quizzed him about drinking coffee, and wearing tinted glasses. Jones eventually explained to him that American black's, no matter their background, have a deep love for Jesus. That is how slavery lasted as it did, because the slave master essentially replaced their true religions and cultures with a passive Christian idol whom they could emulate. Now, many blacks are of the mind that they'll get their just due when they die and go to heaven. It's something I picked up from the Willie Lynch letter. Roberts reminded him that it didn't work on Blackwell. The only conclusion he could come up with was the psychological chains of slavery had been broken.

"So, who's next on our list of Allah worshippers?"

"Let's see. How about we place a dog tag on Mr. Mckenzie?"

It was more than a month before they located Frederick Mckenzie. It was worth the wait, because Jones had to tie up a few loose ends and try to wrap this case around his mind. He never rushed anything, he always left people with enough rope to hang themselves. He hoped Mr. McKenzie's rope was long enough.

"Howdy Mr. Frederick Mckenzie." Said Detective Roberts.

"What's up?"

"You seem comfortable, you been here awhile?

"Yeah, like two hours."

"we're not keeping you from anything are we?"

"Naaah, I was chillin like a penguin."

"Did you know your head is bigger than your body? That means, you think you're going to get out of this."

"Whatever man."

"Oh I'm sorry for being rude, my name is detective Jack Roberts; that's sir to you."

"That's funny."

"You think that's funny, wait til I pin the murder of Damian Johnson on you – ha, ha, ha to that."

"That's cute, but you know what's really funny? I want my lawyer. Ha, ha, ha to that, Mr. Mckenzie." Said Detective Jones. "Let's be reasonable. We want to talk about this without those pesky attorneys. Here, let's try this, do you believe in Jesus Christ?"

"Yeah, why?"

"Well, let me pray for you and then we'll sit and talk like reasonable adults."

"Hell nah. I want a fuckin attorney, I don't want to hear no prayers and shit. Get me an attorney or take me to jail."

"Alright, if that's the way you want it."

Both detectives got up and walked out the door. Detective Roberts reminded Jones that his prayer wasn't working, and suggested that he get another prayer or start questioning if these guys are black. They discussed the prayer tactic for awhile, then Jones had to remind him that word on the street that they're on to whoever did the murder. Jones knew they were talking to each other trying to get their stories together. Sooner or later someone would fold, they just had to be patient. It had been about two weeks when the police picked up Joe Espinoza from school and brought him to the police station for questioning. They placed Joe in a room with a plastic chair and wooden table with the heat turned up, and watched him through the two way mirror.

"Look, he's getting impatient, yeah, this is our guy." Said Detective Jones. Joe looked up at them as they entered the room.

"Heeey Amiiigo, como esta? Or is it mi casa, su casa?" Said Detective Roberts.

Joe leaned back, trying not to reveal his irritation and said, "what the hell are you talkin about?"

"I'm talkin about Damian Johnson."

"Who's that?"

"Who's that. Come on amigo, you know who it is."

"First of all, I'm not an amigo, gringo."

"I apologize, but you are sure going to be cooked like a taco when I send you to prison for murder, retardo."

Joe sat there smiling and shaking his head.

"It's funny, ain't it? You know, I have an entire vocabulary of words in el spanol, that means prison, locked up, and incarcerated. You know how to say, don't drop the soap?"

"Look, we're here to solve a murder that occurred several months back, and we need to know who did it. If you know and you're afraid to tell us, we can get you money and relocate your family. But you have to be truthful. It's a win-win for you."

"I don't know what you're talkin about. In fact, quiero un abagado; in English, that means, I want a lawyer."

Detective Roberts looked at his partner with a look of disbelief, then they abruptly walked out of the interrogation room, as they did with all uncooperative interrogates and headed back to the office. "How can you be so laid back while these punks are runnin around the city shootin up people?" Said Detective Roberts.

Detective Jones responded smoothly, "All we need is a little patience.

Pointing at him disbelief. "Look at you with your feet kicked up like that little fucker just didn't walk out the door scot free. He's probably still sittin there like an idiot."

Roberts took a sip of his chamomile tea, leaned further back in his chair and said, "Like I told you before, just be patient, the Lord's prayer will work."

Three days after Joe was questioned by detectives Robert and Jones he stood listening to Fred opening the goal. Vino started talking about the detectives investigating Damian's murder. He told everyone to ensure that they lawyered up, because the Roman soldiers are tricky and diabolical, from that day on, they would have goals once a month unless it was an emergency. Since it was a school year, everyone should stay busy with school projects and spend time in the house, and to stay away from any parties or events where the particular ones could possibly be. After the goal, everyone sat and talked for a while. Once everyone was done hanging out, they went their separate ways to await next month's meeting.

Joe and James left together. "Did the police talk to you?" asked Joe.

"Nah."

"Alright, you're in the clear, just kick back and we'll see each other at school or meet on Fridays at my crib if we can."

"Yeah, that'll give me time to hang with Zaria. Plus, my dad's been actin suspicious when I show up late."

"Well, don't worry, everything is cool. All the stuff is in the river or I burned it. Once they arrived at Joe's, James headed home to relax a little. On the walk home James though about what happened to Damian, he didn't like the fact that Damian took David's bullet. He didn't see him until the last second, how was he supposed to know? He got in the way of the gun, it was over and that was that. That night, he talked to Zaria for a few hours and made plans to see her that weekend. It wasn't much to do after bible study, so James went to his dad's office and grabbed the bible to look up the Lord's prayer. Then said some detective was saying to them until they got to asking for lawyers.

That month, James hung out with Zaria and spent time in her bedroom when the house was empty. He studied some lit Vino gave him and reviewed the meanings of the top hat, cane, and glove. He thought about getting a tattoo of the three, but decided against it. That's all it would take for his dad to see it, and all hell would break loose. James couldn't believe how fast the month had went by as he stood there listening to the usual discussion at the goal. Rico was out the hospital, he looked a hundred percent better. Rico showed everyone his knife wounds; they weren't that bad, most of the stab wounds were in his legs. James reminded himself to talk to Rico about runnin where he's supposed to and stay away from Co Co's house.

That month came and went. It was getting chilly out, and winter was approaching faster than usual, it seemed that way to James as he ordered a whopper with no bacon. James turned to go to his seat an accidentally bumped into a man standing next to him.

"Excuse me." Said James.

In a hostile tone, the guy said "Yeah, you're excused."

"Who you talkin to?"

"You, you little gang-bangin punk. You guys come up here every day and make noise, and take all the seats so no one can sit down. "

James sat there listening to the guy and said "fuck you" and threw his drink at the guy. The guy threw a punch at James and caught him in the mouth. James backed up in a fightin stance. The man rushed James with a fury of blows, James met him with the same zeal. Joe saw James fighting, ran over and hit the guy with a food tray, as he leaned forward from the blow.

Ray picked up a plastic garbage can and hit him with it, he fell to the ground and struggled to get up, but James caught him with a kick in the face. As he fell back, Joe followed up with another kick to the side of his head. James started stomping on him until they heard the police say "Don't move!"

James and Joe sat in the back of the squad car. Joe was screaming "fuck you!" and James was tellin them to take him to the hospital because his mouth wouldn't stop bleeding. The responses to his request were denied with a shut up. At the juvenile detention center, James was looked at by a nurse who told him he would be o.k., he just had a busted lip and it didn't stop bleeding because his adrenaline was pumpin, which cause the wound to bleed more. James and Joe sat in a holding room until their parents come to pick them up. Joe's dad arrived first.

A guard told James he had a special visit. He was escorted down the hall to a room with a large conference table and leather chairs around the table. As he leaned back in the chair thinking about how comfortable it was. Detective Roberts and Jones walked in.

"Heeey little buddy. I see you're a prize fighter, you like beating up on hard working citizens in Minnesota. Oooh, looks like your lip got the best of the fight." Said Detective Roberts.

"I was hit by a grown man, and you tryin to lock me up? I didn't do anything."

Detective Roberts leaned close to James and said, "Listen Sugar Ray, I don't give a fuck if he beat your brains out the back of your skull; I'm here to talk to you about this little fella here."

As he slid a picture of Damian's corpse across the table for James to see. James leaned back and said "I don't know who that is."

"Sure you do. This is your handy work. Here you are getting arrested with Mr. Espinoza and you don't know who this guy is. I'm willing to bet you were there when Bishop was shot."

James leaned back and let out a sigh and said, "If you say so."

"Where were you when Bishop was shot?"

"Nowhere."

"Who can verify your no-where-ness?"

James sarcastically said, "God can."

Detective Jones chimed in, "You believe in God, James?"

"Yeah, why not?

"It is customary for me to say the Lord's prayer in all interrogations. To let people know life is a struggle and we all have faults, and God will forgive you if you repent."

"Oh, you mean Psalm 23." James sarcastically recited the prayer without any mistakes.

Detective Jones looked at James amusingly, deep inside he was shocked this kid knew the prayer – he's the smart one out of the bunch, Jones thought.

Detective Roberts clapped after James recited the prayer. "You are a real tool, you know that?"

"I don't know what a tool is, but whenever I ask for my lawyer I recite the Al Fatihah, you wanna hear it?

Jones and Roberts left James in the conference room wondering when they were going to come back. They headed to the office and hung James mug shot next to: Fred, Vino, and Joe's. These were the primes suspects, they would sit back and wait until they made another mistake. Detective Jones leaned back in his chair sippin chamomile tea, looking at the four pictures, thinking, though I walk through the valley of the shadow of death.

Later that evening James sat at the living room table explaining to his dad what happened at Burger King. His dad told him not to leave school at lunch to avoid the non-sense. As James listened to his dad's instructions, he wondered why he didn't ask him about the homicide detectives questioning him. He thought, if he doesn't say anything, I'm not bringing it up. After they were done talking, James laid in bed with an ice pack on his mouth thinkin, if he had that .38, somebody wouldn't really needed the Lord's prayer.

CHAPTER NINE

A LOSS IN THE FAMILY

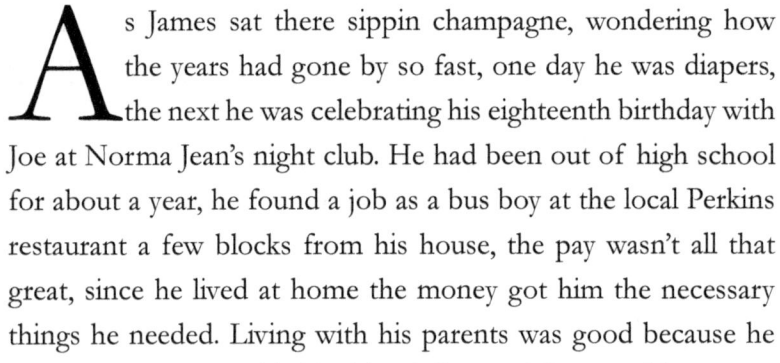

As James sat there sippin champagne, wondering how the years had gone by so fast, one day he was diapers, the next he was celebrating his eighteenth birthday with Joe at Norma Jean's night club. He had been out of high school for about a year, he found a job as a bus boy at the local Perkins restaurant a few blocks from his house, the pay wasn't all that great, since he lived at home the money got him the necessary things he needed. Living with his parents was good because he needed a car to go with his driver's license. The way things were going, he'd have the money sooner or later.

The last few years seemed hectic, the detective's stopped snooping around, but it was always some drama with someone in the crew. The upside was, he learned so much lit, that Vino put him in charge of teaching other brothas the meaning behind what they were reciting and how to live in accordance with those principles. He and Joe always hung out, the only time they weren't together was when James had to work or he had some business to handle with Zaria. Now, they were celebrating his birthday together at Norma Jean's. Since Norma Jean's hosted an eighteen plus teen night, that was the best option. With Fred, Vino, and Cedric being there, the champagne wasn't a problem, the other plus was Dominque was a bouncer at the club, so the coast was clear

That was the first time Zaria had been around James' friends outside of the incident when she helped them get away from the skirmish downtown. He made sure to stay close to Zaria so she wouldn't accuse him of being around other girls. For the rest of the night, James and Joe celebrated their birthdays, though Joe's birthday was in August. It was cool, it gave James a reason to celebrate in August. They had become close since the incident with Damian, though they were layin low as much as possible, they weren't sweatin the detective's because, after all, they were the key to the door they wanted to unlock. As James sat there sippin his drink, Joe slurred, "Happy birthday bruh, I love you man."

"Thanks bruh, next month we're doin this again."

"Shit, we should do this every day. Look at all these girls, damn."

Pointing at Zaria, James said "This is the only girl for me bruh."

"Whelp, I'm single and ready to mingle"; he smiled, lifted his glass and slurred, "to the family.

While James stood there placing spoons in the utensil holder, he glanced at Lisa as she walked by. He had forgotten he promised to show her around Minneapolis, since she was relatively new to the city. Lisa was cool, but with her short sandy brown hair, light brown eyes, and an hourglass figure that complimented her small breasts and a waist that was even smaller that accentuated her butt, he couldn't let Zaria his plans of showing Lisa around, or he'd never hear the end of it. As she walked to waiting customers, James thought, she has a big butt for a white girl. Lisa had been working at Perkins a year before James was hired. She told him she had moved from Fargo, North Dakota, and had the accent to prove it. She and James talked a lot about Minneapolis, though she had been in Minneapolis a few years, she didn't venture out much.

James promised her he would show her around whenever he had free time. He really meant, whenever Zaria was working, he knew she wouldn't believe she was a friend or coworker in the last. Lisa broke his thought as she entered the kitchen and said, "Hey, what's up James?"

He looked over his shoulder while he was spraying food off dishes. "What's happenin' Miss North Dakota?"

"Oh, just chillin, as you put it."

"Don't chill too much or you might get a cold."

She walked close to James and said, "I hope I have you to keep me warm."

"Yeah, I'll be your blanket."

"Is that all you have to keep me warm?" Pointing at her butt, Lisa said, "You know I have all this, so you're going to need a lot more thank a blanket."

James thought, damn, that is a whole lot to keep warm; and said, "anything is possible."

"Anyway, you promised me a movie, when are we going to go?"

"I think I promised to show you around."

"I want to see a movie."

"I have to check my schedule."

"You mean, you have to ask that girl that drops you off at work sometimes."

"Who, Zaria?"

"Yeah."

"That's my girl."

"I guess she has you on a leash."

"Nah, she just goes crazy if she see's me with other females."

"Well, she won't hear it from me."

"Ain't that something?"

"Why'd you say that?"

"Cuz most women can't keep a secret."

Making a cross across her chest she said, "I promise to God."

"Oh, you believe in God, huh?"

"Of course."

"Do you know the Lord's prayer?"

"No, but I can learn it."

James laughed and said, "Never mind. We'll get together next Sunday, Zaria has to work that night so I'll take you to a movie, and get you home safe before Zaria gets off work."

"O.k., where do you want to meet?"

"Here's the best place. Since I don't work on the Lord's Day and you do, we can meet here."

"It's a date, and you better be here" and Lisa, as she turned and walked to wait her table.

Three days after Joe celebrated James' birthday, he sat looking at Detectives Roberts and Jones. "Look you little shit. Or is it mirs tu comemierda? I've been polishing up on my espanol, we've finally gotchu." Said Detective Jones. Joe sat there staring at Detective Jones as if he were a moron. It's been awhile, but I knew you would do something stupid. Now your ass is mine."

Joe leaned back and said, "The last time we met, I told you quiero unabogado, didn't i?"

Leaning close to Joe, Jones said in a menacing tone, "And I told you, locked up, in jail, and incarcerated, didn't I?"

"Whatever."

"Did you really think you could shoot two people in a night club parking lot, and get away with it? You don't have your friends to protect this time."

"If I may interrupt. Mr. Espinoza, you know I recite the Lord's prayer to all the people I interview."

Joe interrupted, "I don't want to hear no fuckin prayer."

"Well, how about how we let you go if you tell us about Damian Robinson?"

"I'm not talkin about anything, but why my attorney isn't here pinche Puerco."

"Since I'm a pinche Puerco, I'll pass and let the guards take you back to your cell – ten un bwen dia," said Detective Jones as he and Detective Roberts left the interrogation room. While walking down the hall, detective Roberts said, "We got him, all we have to do is keep at him."

"Why?"

"So the case can get reversed on appeal, when they find out we were pressing him after he invoked his right to counsel."

"Who are they going to believe, him or us?"

"I'm not willing to bet on it, so we'll have to wait. Besides, the people he shot took bullets to the arm and leg – he'll get a decent please, this is his first offense. We'll catch him on the next one."

"James, telephone," said Andrew. James got off the couch wondering who was callin him.

"Hello."

"Hey James, what's up?" said Chelle.

"Oh hey Chelle, what's goin on?"

"I'm callin to let you know that Joe is in jail."

"What happened?"

"He went to Norma Jean's after the goal, got into it with somebody, and shot two people."

"Who was there with him?"

"Nobody, Dominique was workin that night, that's how Vino found out."

"What they tryin to do to him?"

"We don't know yet."

"Alright, I'll talk to his brother and see what's up. I'll see you on Friday." James hung up the phone thinking, I just saw him a few days ago and told him not to go to Norma Jeans. James sat back on the couch thinkin, fuck, how'd he get in that shit; I told his ass not to go.

That Sunday, Lisa came out of the locker room with a pair of jeans on that favored her butt so much James couldn't help but think, hoooly shit. "Let's go" said Lisa.

James gave her directions to a movie theater on Lake Street; it was close to Baskin Robbins, he wanted to go there after the movie. James leaned back in the front seat listening to Lisa talk about the job, her future plans to start college so she could get a better payin job. He agreed while directing her to the theater.

A few hours later, Lisa said, "that was alright," as they left the theater heading to the car. "Where to now?"

"I have a surprise, get in."

James directed her to drive three blocks to the Baskin Robbins. In a disappointed tone, Lisa said, "ice cream?"

"What, it's thirty one flavors."

"I have ice cream at home."

"Ice cream is ice cream, ain't it?"

"Well. My ice cream is free."

"So whatchu wanna do? We can go to a restaurant or something; Wendy's is up the street."

"How about ice cream at my place?"

"Whatever you want Miss North Dakota."

As Lisa opened the door to her apartment, she excitedly said, "this is it."

James entered, looked around, and thought this is nice. As she went to the kitchen, she said, "Have a seat, let me go get the ice cream. You can turn on the T.V. if you want. James leaned back on the sofa thinking, this is really nice, a comfortable couch, soft clean carpet. I can't wait to get my own place.

"Here you go, I hope you like vanilla."

"Vanilla's cool, thanks."

James could see Lisa changed into a pair of sweat pants and a bigger T-shirt. "it's good ain't it?"

"Yeah, all ice cream is good, but Baskin Robbins still has thirty-one flavors."

"It doesn't matter, I would've ordered vanilla anyway. So why waste money on something I already have?"

"That makes sense. But a little strawberry ice cream with chocolate chips in it wouldn't hurt."

"You like that flavor?" Lisa sat her bowl of ice cream down on the living room table, leaned over and lightly took James' bowl of ice cream, sat it on the table next to hers and said, "tell me how this tastes." She took a bite of ice cream, sat the bowl back on the table, turned to James and kissed him sliding her tongue in his mouth so he could taste the ice cream. "Is it good?"

"Umm hummm." Lisa began kissing him again, running her tongue down his neck, taking off his shirt; she then licked his bare chest and let her tongue slide to his stomach. Lisa could feel the bulge in James' pants as she unzipped them. As James leaned back with his pants pulled down to his ankles, he could feel the warmth of Lisa's tongue as her mouth went up and down his penis. James leaned back thinking, this is impossible as he placed his hand on top of Lisa's head so he could control the pace of her head while she sucked his penis. Lisa stopped, got off her knees and said, "come on."

James followed her to her bedroom, with is pants around his ankles. Lisa pulled off her shirt, James saw her erect nipples; as she took off her sweatpants James saw her panties were gone and to his surprise she had no hair. James excitedly undressed and got in the bed. Lisa slowly mounted him, he could feel her wetness as she leaned forward and slid up and down on his penis. James firmly gripped her butt so he could control rhythm of her movement. The only thing James could this was, this feels soooo good, he thought that for the rest of the night.

The next morning, Lisa lay there asleep while James looked at her body thinking, this is gorgeous. Man, I can't believe this. I might be like my Uncle Kenny after all as he smiled. At Friday's goal, Dominique explained the incident with Joe. James stood there listening in disbelief; he couldn't believe Joe would do something so stupid. He knew Joe was a hot head, with liquor added, that made the situation worse. He didn't have to shoot up the parking lot like he was a cowboy – he has to get out of this somehow.

"Who's snitchin on him?" asked Ray.

"From what we know, the people who were shot weren't the people he was arguing with. They were innocent bystanders tryin to get out of the way," said Dominique.

"It's pretty much a dead situation. That many people watchin him shoot up the place; there's plenty of witnesses, way too many for us to talk to. It's a sad situation when you're off your square and make a crucial slip. It not only cost him, but it cost us – it's a serious loss to the family," said Vino.

CHAPTER TEN

LOYAL TO THE GAME

Six months after Joe's arrest, James stood at the goal explain Lordism and it's authenticity. "Thank you," said Vino as he shook his head in agreement. "This is who we are and how we live, we don't discriminate, we are not prejudice, we love and honor those who love and honor us. Make no mistake about it, we are not one of those loose street nigga's with no goals or principles. We stand tall in the eyes of Allah and honor our positions as vicegerents of this earth. Alright, Louie close it out."

James stood there with his palms raised as Louie closed the goal. He was surprise that Louie knew it, he always smoked weed and acted like a burn out. After the goal, James stayed and played quarters; since he wasn't a big drinker, he made sure he played his hand carefully. Though he enjoyed himself, he couldn't help but think about Joe getting five and a half years for the shooting at the club. I guess that's what his P.D. called a deal, James thought as he played his card. He kept thinking, of all the scenarios he could that wouldn't kept Joe out of trouble had he been there. The more he ran the scenarios through his mind, the more he though Joe's ass is crazy. He would've definitely went off. He didn't know if Joe would be cool in prison, he was sure to get into something, he'd shoot him a letter to keep in touch, he thought as he turned up a shot of peach schnapps.

That evening James lay next to Zaria thinking about Lisa. He wondered what it would be like to be with her again. She acted like nothing happened while they were at work, but she always told him to come over. Though he was hesitant, he couldn't say no. He smirked and thought, that girl is a mess.

James opened the letter from Joe. He noticed it had a St. Cloud return address on it. He sat wondering, where the hell St. Cloud was, he thought it was South of Minneapolis, wherever it was, it was too far to have Joe locked up. He laughed when he saw Joe had gotten a little bigger from lifting weights, as he read the letter he figured Joe was cool, at least for being in the hole. He shook his head and when he read: these motha fucka's in here are stupid bruh. It's cool though because all I do is beat them down. I only have a few years left, it may seem like a lot, but when you're in here, it goes by fast. He continued giving James the details of prison life, the CO's, the chow hall, the fucked up phones, and all the skirmishes he got into. He was keeping himself busy, thought James. It's the same Joe, don't start none won't be none. But knowing Joe, he started it. James laughed to himself on his way to work about Joe's letter, he'd be sure to write him back when he got home. As he came out of the locker room, Lisa said "what's up James?"

"I'm cool, what's up with you?"

She turned around and arched her back and said, "this."

"Yeah, that's what's up." James said with a smile, as he reached out to touch her butt.

She quickly moved away. "Not at work, you know the rules. Are you coming over tonight?"

"I'll see if I can make it."

"You said that last time."

"You know Zaria might call or come over. If I'm not around, she'll go crazy and start drillin me. I'm not tryin to hear her naggin at me."

"Why don't you leave her. I don't bother you, you can do whatever you want, just be home when the sun sets."

Shaking his head in disbelief, James said, "Man you're something else."

"Well, when are you coming over?"

"How's Sunday?"

"How about tonight?"

"Did you just ask me when I was comin over?"

Lisa sighed, rolled her eyes, and said "Zaria or whatever her name is works all week except Saturday, so you can come over."

"Yep, but I get together with her after she gets off work. Don't worry, I'll be there Sunday."

"Whatever." Lisa said, as she turned and walked up the stairs to wait tables.

James split the time between Zaria and Lisa, and prayed Zaria didn't find out about Lisa. It would be a serious situation. He decided to tell Lisa that he couldn't mess with anymore. But decided against it, he figured Lisa would get mad because he rejected her. It was a situation he'd figure out, until then, they would have to share.

A year had passed since Joe was in prison. James wrote him once a month, whether he heard from Joe or not. The last letter Joe was doing good and getting a vocation in brick laying and stayin outta trouble. He told James the Brotha's are on point, and he learned a lot from them. Joe was never good at remembering lit, but he had plenty of time to study so he was using it to his benefit. The relationship he shared with Zaria and Lisa didn't change. He put together a schedule, so he wouldn't have to make Zaria suspicious; he was always with the brotha's or his dad. Besides, Lisa just wanted to sit in her apartment and chill with him, that eliminated any accidental run-ins with Zaria.

Friday's goals had been once a week, since the murder investigation was pretty much over. Though James thought about it often, especially since Joe wrote in his letter, that the dick-heads had been to see him. He didn't worry because if Joe didn't tell, it was a dead end. He thought, that's the beauty of loyalty.

A few weeks later Zaria stood in front of her house listening to James talk about the features on his 1987 maroon Malibu. She thought it looked nice, but he over did it with runnin his hand over the cars roof callin it his baby. James said excitedly, "look, the upholstery is like silk", while he ran his hand over the seat. "You can't find this nowhere in America."

"Looks more like soft pleather to me."

"Ahhh, so you're a non-believer. Get in and I'll show you."

Zaria got in the front seat and James sat in the driver's seat. "Feels like soft pleather." Said Zaria and started laughin.

"Nah girl, I'll bet your ass ain't never felt nothin that soft and silky."

"I can think of a few things."

"Yeah, my hands on that ass."

"That's real funny. Where are we going?"

"Nowhere, we're going to sit here and enjoy this supa fly Llac."

"This ain't no Llac."

"Yeah it is. You have to imagine that it is."

"Well, I'm imagining that we're driving somewhere."

"Where you wanna go."

"Let's go to Lake Nokomis."

James laughed and said, "Imagine that."

"That's real funny, stop playin, let's go to the lake."

James turned the engine over and said "Say it loud, I'm black and I'm proud, oooh wee." They drove to Lake Nokomis and enjoyed the view, people swimming, joggin, and walking their dogs. "Man, I like it over here. Look at these houses."

"Yeah, they're nice."

James pointing at a big brown house with white trim said, "Imagine livin in that."

"Yep, just us two."

"What about kids?"

Mimicking Arnold from A Different Strokes, James said, "Whatchu talkin about, Willis?"

"What, you don't want kids?"

"Are you pregnant or something?"

"No. You know I've been on the pill for years."

"Whoo, I thought you were going to tell me you were pregnant."

"I'm sure that'd be cool, but we don't have big house money."

"If we keep working, we'll have it."

"Maybe." While Zaria kept talking about having a family and a big house, James thought that would be impossible with Lisa around. Maybe I should end it, but why, it's working out so far. Besides, we're not finna have a family anytime soon. "Do you hear me James?" said Zaria as she interrupted his thought.

"Yeah, I hear you."

"What'd I say then?"

"What you said."

"That's funny."

James looked at her with a smirk on his face and said, "What, you don't remember what you said?" He shook his head at her look, smiled, and started the car so he could drop her off at home, head to work, then to Lisa's.

Thirteen hours later James was holding back as he hovered above Lisa listening to her say, "uh, uh, uh, uh ,oh James, hush," as he hovered between her legs thrusting until he felt himself tremble from an orgasm.

Out of breath, Lisa lightly licked James nipple and said, "I love when you come over."

Breathing heavy, James responded, "I love cumming too. What time is it?"

"Don't worry about the time."

"I have somewhere to be."

"Where you going? It's still early."

"It's just an appointment with my people."

"It's not that bitch with the funny name is it?"

"What are you talkin about?"

"That bitch."

"Come on. Stop callin Zaria bitches, she doesn't call you bitches."

"Oh, I'm a bitch now?"

"You know what I mean."

"I hope I know whatchu mean."

"Listen, I gotta go."

"So, where you goin?"

"I gotta go get Louie, if you need to know. I told him I'd make a quick run with him."

"Can I go?"

Looking at her in disbelief, James said, "N-O."

"Oh, now you don't want to be seen with me."

"Nah."

"What?"

James laughed. "Your butt might bring too much unneeded attention."

"Ha ha really funny."

"Get up, I gotta get ready."

James stood in the shower thinking he couldn't believe she was sweatin him like that, damn. She's a trip. How'd I get myself caught up in this? Shit, I guess this is a man's world an it wouldn't be nothin without a woman or a girl. As he headed out the door James said, "Alright, I'll be back later."

I'll be here waitin." Said Lisa and opened her robe to show James what would be waitin for him.

Thirty minutes later, James pulled up to C's house and honked the horn for Louie to come out. Louie got in the car, closed the door and said, "Damn bruh, I though you would never show up."

"I had to take care of some business," said James as he backed out the drive way."

"What up tho?"

"Man, chillin like a penguin. Tryin to dodge these crazy females."

"that's what I'm talkin about."

"The shit is crazy bruh. Two jealous females is a lot of stress."

"How you stressin over two pieces of pussy, that's a virgin's dream."

I'm not really stressin like that. They just want to hound me about this or that, I got it handled though."

"You better putcha playa boots on bruh."

"That's funny." As they drove, James thought about his Uncle Kenny's playa from the Himalayas line. Louie interrupted his thought when James heard him say, "Ain't that David." Looking around to see if he could David, James responded, "Yep, that's him and some of them marks he be with.

Louie pulled out a .380 out of his jacket pocket, laid it across his lap and said, "Hit the block again." As James circled the block he asked where Louie where he went. "He was by the brick house in the middle of the block."

James drove by the house, but he didn't see anyone. "Hit the alley bruh." James took a left and drove down the alley. "Slow down, there he is, drive by him and let me out by that garage."

As Louie opened the car door to get out, he turned and told James to drive two blocks over, park, and he'd meet him there.

When James pulled out of the alley, he drove to the spot to wait on Louie, several seconds later, James heard four shots.

Damn, that little .380 is loud, he thought while he was parked, engine running, waitin for Louie. The wait seemed like an eternity. He looked into his rearview mirror and saw Louie casually walking up the block. Louie calmly got into the car and said, "Take me to River Road."

James headed to Wet River Parkway, they call it River Road for short, it was a few spots along the Mississippi River James and Joe used to hang at and drink beers and shoot guns at the edge of the river. Louie sat in the passenger seat with the .380 in his lap in case the police got behind them. He was always good at jumpin out of cars when the police got behind a car he was in, in fact, he was good at runnin from the police period, James thought as he drove away from the police sirens in the distance.

Once they got to River Road, Louie told James to pull over. He got out and disappeared into a thick of trees. James waited for a few minutes and Louie reappeared from the same trees he disappeared into. "Let's go to my crib," said Louie as he put his Minnesota Twins baseball cap on and leaned back into the passenger seat. On the drive to Louie's, James listened to music and wasn't concerned about asking Louie who had been shot, or where he hid the gun. Vino taught James it's not good to know everyone, most importantly, loose lips sink ships. They arrived at Louie's got out, and went in. James sat on the dark maroon couch and waited on Louie to get back from the bathroom. Louie came into the living room with his five year old son Melvin following.

"Hey little man" said James.

"Hi, what's your name?" said Melvin

"I'm James."

"Where are you from James?"

Teasing Melvin, James said, "I'm from everywhere."

Looking confused, Melvin said, "I'm five."

"That's cool, I'm a bunch of fives that make up twenty."

Louie interrupted. "Hey, Elaine, come and get Mel. Alright Mel, go in the kitchen with your mom. Daddy has to talk to James." As Melvin headed into the kitchen, Louie and James went to the enclosed porch, shut the double doors behind them, and sat down on the sofa's that wrapped around the porch with a big square table at the center. "This is my smokin room." Louis said as he rolled up a joint. He lit the joint, took a long drag, and passed it to James. Coughing, James said, "What's in this shit?"

"This is from the Rez bruh. You ain't gonna get nothin better, unless you go to a weed planet." Jams took another drag and coughed again. Louie reached out and said, "let me get that, you're baby sittin. I think this might be too much for you."

James passed on another puff. As he sat there listening to Louie describe all the different kinds of weed, he felt his body relax, his eyes get heavy, and his lips seemed to keep drooping. He was high, and he could feel it. James didn't smoke or drink much; when he did, it was usually with one of the brothas – he avoided not being sober in public. It was his own interpretation of, to be aware is to be alive.

He sat there for a few hours talkin to Louie about earning some extra cash that wouldn't et him into a bind with the police. After their conversation, James decided to go home. The drive seemed long; he rolled down his window so that the breeze would keep him alert as he drove. On the way home, he made a detour to Lisa's; James remembered she had something under that silk robe for him.

The next morning, he showered, dressed, and headed home. Thirty minutes later, he sat at the kitchen table eating cereal. His mom came into the kitchen and greeted James, he responded with his usual "What up?"

"Nothin, just finna have my daily coffee. Where were you last night, I didn't see your car?"

"At a friends."

"Well, I hope you have a name for that friend because Zaria called a few times and came over."

"For real? That girl is crazy."

"Well, you better have an excuse, or she might go crazy on you."

"Nah, she's cool. We go through this all the time, if she didn't do it, I'd think something was wrong with her."

Taking a sip of coffee Pat said, "make sure you're not playin both sides of the fence. If it's another girl, you better make a choice."

James sat there thinking, she is right, but I can't help it. I want both of them. Lisa knows I have a girl and she wants to be with me. Shit, the coast is clear. All I have to do is calm Zaria down. As his mom headed upstairs, she said, "Well, I'll leave you to your thoughts." James finished eating, went upstairs and slept.

A few hours later, his mom shook him awake. "James, Zaria's on the phone." He looked around, still tired, and made his way to the phone. In a groggy voice, he said, "hello."

"What's up?"

"Shit, chillin."

"I was callin you all night, what happened?"

"Smokin weed is what happened."

"What do you mean?"

"I went to Louie's, smoked some weed, and crashed until today. I'm still kinda tired from that shit."

"How come you didn't call me?"

"I didn't know I had to."

"Why you always getting smart?"

"I didn't know I was supposed to call you is not getin smart, it's a comment. Did you tell me to call you?"

"Whatever."

James said angrily, "Answer the question." Zaria sat there in silence. Raising his voice James said, "Hello?"

"I—" James slammed the phone down before she could say anything. As he turned to walk away, the phone range. He answered it and it was Zaria on the other end. Screaming at James she said, "why'd you hang up on me?"

"Bye Zaria, I'll talk to you later," said James as he hung up the phone. He left he phone off the receiver in case she called back. James thought, he'd get some rest, drive to her house, and see what was up with her. That evening, James and Zaria sat in his car at Lake Nokomis talking. She did most of the talking while James leaned back and agreed with whatever she said. He learned that debating with women did not work. That was something he learned from his dad. Whenever his mom had a point to make, his dad would say, yes dear. Though, he didn't say yes dear, he made sure he acknowledged what she was saying and paid attention to her questions because he tended to blank out whenever she nagged him. To preserve their relationship, and to keep from slippin up with his lies, he paid close attention and answered only if it was a question. After talking with Zaria, they decided to walk around the lake. It was a cool light summer breeze, the lake was full of people taking and evening jog, or walk. He paid attention to the orange glow of the sun setting on the horizon, and its reflection off the water. He stayed lost in his thoughts a she walked holding hands with Zaria. After the walk around the lake, they went to a motel, James' treat.

The past several months were hectic. James juggled two relationships, a job, and kept Zaria as calm as he could. It was always something with her. Whenever he talked to Lisa about it, she would call her a bitch or a needy bitch. James stopped responding to her comments because it would only cause them to argue. Since it was winter, James had plenty of excuses, and he got his supervisor to give him more hours at work because he was saving for an apartment and he had to pay for the little bills he had. The extra hours kept him busy, and away from Lisa and Zaria. He split his off days between both of them, since Zaria worked longer hours than Lisa that was a plus to James. He could spend a few more hours with Lisa and a few more hours with Zaria. He attended goals twice a month because he had to work most Fridays> There were a few new brotha's in the fold, James hung out with them a few times, but his schedule precluded him from going to parties or any extra activities that he used to do when he didn't have a job, and two women to deal with. He enjoyed it, yet, it was still a game of juggling. It had been a few months since James had been out; since it was Friday, he headed to the goal> James sat on the couch at Vino's talking to Louis about the Rez dro James responded, "Man, I've been layin low, chillin. Besides, that shit put me asleep fro two days.

"I told you the stuff I have is phenomenal bruh. Whatchu finna get into tonight?"

"I was thinkin after goal I might head over to Zaria's and see what she's up to."

"Nah, fuck that. Let's go to this part over North."

"I'm cool, I don't mess around over there too much."

"it's a brotha's party."

"You know I don't too much fuck with them. Ever since Colors came out, them nigga's been flippin crip."

"It's Marshawn's party, he one-hundred V.L."

"Who's all going?

Pointing at everyone, "We all going bruh."

"Alright, let's ride then."

James drove to the party on Bryant with Louie, Chelle, and Cassandra in his car, while everyone else piled in the other two cars. They arrived, got out, walked to the white house on a hill. James could hear the music, that let him know he was at the right location. Louie introduced James to Duane, who was manning the front door. James shook hands with Duane and made his way into the party, he saw people dancing, leaning on the walls talking, and plenty of girls running around.

The friend chicken and beer had a distinct smell; it was hard to describe, but James knew it was a real house party if it had a combination of the two. He bobbed his head to the music, and was shocked to see a D.J. and turntables. Most parties, you never knew where the music came from. You just saw large speakers sittin in a corner.

James was offered a beer. He passed because it was a different environment, even though he noticed a lot of brotha's in the party. He saw Reggie flag him in his direction. James weaved through the crowd, Reggie introduced him to Marshawn, they shook up and began to talk.

"This is Tim, Bilal, and Meril," said Marshawn, as he introduced James to the brotha's that were standing there. They began to talk, James found out they were from the West Side of Chicago. And had been living in Minnesota for a few years. While talking, James invited them to attend goals over South. Marhsawn agreed to be there the following Friday. They sat and talked for a minute; James decided to get some air, with the heat on, and all the bodies in the party, he felt hot and closed in. Though it was a chilly winter night, the cold air felt good. As James leaned on the windowless frame of the inside porch, four guys walked up the steps and tried to get into the party. Duane turned them away, letting them know it was a private party. They took the rejection as an insult, and started calling Duane names.

Duane told them, "Get the fuck away from here." A skinny light skinned guy with bug eyes said, "fuck you bitch ass nigga." As Duane walked in their direction, James topped him.

"Fuck you nigga," said a brown-skinned guy with long braids.

"Whatever," James responded.

"I know it's whatever."

"listen, we're just here chillin, why don't ya'll go somewhere," said James.

"Make us go somewhere," said the light skinned guy. Duane charged down the stairs and threw a punch at the light skinned guy that spun him when it connected. Damn, James though as he went to break up the fight. As they fell in the snow, James tried to grab Duane off the light skinned guy who was getting the worst of the fight> As he bent to grab Duane, James felt a blow to his ear, that made his head snap to the side as he hit the snow. He looked up, saw a fat dark skinned guy standing over him, with his fist headed in his direction.

James turned and covered his face, the blow hit his forearm. He then kicked up, felt his foot hit the bigger guys stomach; he knew it was a good kick when he heard him let out a loud umph. James lept to his feet and landed a few blows to the fat guys head. The guy rushed him and put him in a bear hug, and threw him back to the ground. As he bent to drive his fist to James' face, Marshawn ran and jump-kicked him in the side, making him grunt from the blow. As he stumbled to the side, he rushed James again, grabbed him by the collar, threw him to the ground, and began to throw wild punches at him. James kicked up in the air and caught him in the face. He stumbled backwards, and James heard pop, pop, pop, pop, pop, pop, pop, pop. The fat guy stumbled forward and landed on James. "Come on bruh," said Reggie as he helped James get the fat guy off him. They ran to the cars, drove down Bryant, turned on Broadway, and headed to 94.

On the drive, James excitedly asked, "who the fuck was shootin?'

"I don't know bruh. I thought they were shootin at you." Said Reggie.

"Where's Louie?" asked James.

Chelle responded, "He's with C and em."

"What the fuck, is everybody o.k.?"

"Yeah, we're cool." Said Reggie.

"I thought that mothafucka was shootin me."

"Nah, the shots sound like they were comin from behind you. It was too dark, I couldn't tell." Said Reggie.

"As long as we're cool, don't worry about it." Said James as he got on 94 headed to the South Side. James dropped everyone off at Chelle's house and decided to go home. On the drive, he cursed himself for going over North. He was also glad he didn't get shot, damn, he thought, that fat mothafucka was woopin my ass – It's cool, he didn't do too much damage. All he did was slam me and dive on me; that fat mothafucka must've been an Olympic diver or something. What was he thinkin, he could dive on me and knock the wind out of me. James' thought about the fat guy diving on.

Chapter Eleven

Freedom

"This is the victim," said an officer to Detective Roberts.

"I can see that. Is there any witnesses?"

"They took them to the station sir."

"Thank you."

"What do you think Mark?"

"Well, looks like the coroner is going to have a hell of a time getting this one on a gurney."

"Looks like he took four to the chest, and one to the throat, and two to the stomach.

He had a hell of a night."

"It looks like the shots were close range. I think the person was standing a few feet away from him. It's hard to tell with all these footprints in the snow. Is that a body print?"

"Looks like it may have been a wrestling match."

"We'll find out when we talk to the witnesses. Looks like the city's gone mad."

Three days later, Detective Roberts laid out the mug shot of Donald Whitaker, AKA Big-D.

"Here we go."

Looking at the mug shot, detective Jones said, "I see he's from Detroit, huh."

"He's a big son of a bitch -six- two, 260. I see why someone put seven slugs in him."

"What kind of slugs were they?"

"The forensics report said a .9mm."

"It looks like he's been around for awhile, his MO is robbery, robbery, and to mix it up, he does a little assaulting people on the side."

"Pull his associates, so we can start tracking down who did this. In the mean time, let's go to the house where this fiasco started."

An hour later, Detective Jones knocked on the door of the white house with the windowless front porch. Detective Jones knocked on the door. A woman who looked to be in her twenties answered the door.

"Hello, are you Miss Juanita Lawrence?"

"Yes."

"I'm detective Roberts and this is my partner Detective Jones. We're investigating the murder that happened outside of your house, and we'd like to ask you a few questions.

Pulling the door up so they couldn't look inside the house, Juanita said, "Alright, what do you want to know?"

"Is the owner of the home here?" asked Detective Jones.

"I am the owner. My mother left the house when she passed."

"Sorry for the loss," said Detective Roberts. We want you to know what happened and who was here, the night of the murder."

"All I Know is, it was a fight and some dude got killed. I already told the police, I was in the kitchen fryin chicken, so I didn't see anything."

"Can you tell us who was here?"

"No. It was a party, so I didn't know the people."

"So you throw parties without knowing who's in your home."

Rolling her eyes at Detective Roberts she said, with a sarcastic tone, "yes."

"Alright Miss Lawrence, have a good day. Here's my card if you can think of anything." Said detective Jones. As they walked away, Juanita walked in the house, closed the door, sat on the couch next to Marshawn, and gave him the detective's card. He laid it on the small table next to the couch, and reminded himself to throw it away when he was done watchin T.V..

"She knows something." Said Roberts.

"Yeah, that chicken is her alibi too."

"Think we should get a warrant?"

"That would be a waste of time. She didn't see anything, but I think she heard about who did it."

The next few months were busy. As winter turned into spring, they still didn't have any leads on the case. It had been three other murders that winter, and it wasn't summer yet. The case might take a turn for the good, because a person had been arrested who fit the description of a person who was at the party. The detectives headed to their offices at City Hall to pick up a few notes, and headed to the interview room at the county jail. Before they entered the room Detective Jones told Roberts to let him handle the interrogation. A few second slater they entered the interrogation room.

"Hello Mr. Williams. My name is Detective Jones and this is my partner, Detective Roberts." In a sooth tone, he asked if he was comfortable or if he needed anything to drink or eat. Little D requested a cigarette. He had been sittin in the county jail for eight weeks on a murder case, and he needed a cigarette bad. "I can accommodate you, but I'll need something in return. "

"Whatchu want?"

"A little information about a party you attended a while back."

"What about it?

"Hold on, let me get you what you asked for." He looked at Roberts letting him know to go get the cigarette. While Roberts left to get the cigarettes out of his desk drawer they kept for people they interviewed. Jones sat silently sizing Little D up. He knew the silence would make him wonder what he was thinking. He did that, because silence is intimidating, and it works wonders on people who conjure up a lie. "Here you go," Roberts, said as he placed a pack of Newport 100's, a book of matches, and a fresh cup of hot coffee in front of Little D. "Is this good? We have some sandwiches if you want one."

"Nah, this is cool, thanks." Taking a deep breath and letting out a long sigh. Jones explained why he recited the Lords prayer in all interrogations; he held Little D's hand and recited the prayer. "O.k., tell me what happened at the party on Bryant."

Little D began telling him about the altercation, he left out the part when he refused to leave, and left in how he was attacked. "Alright, so this guy attacked you outta nowhere?"

"Yeah, I turned around, the next thing I knew, he was on top of me."

"O.k. so how'd Mr. Whitaker get killed?"

"I don't really know. I was getting jumped by two people; I heard some shots and ran. I thought they were shootin at me." I didn't know Big- D was dead until two days later.

Detective Jones rubbed his goatee, pretending to be thinking about what he said and asked.

"Who else was with you?"

"Um, Nate an L."

"Do you know their real names?

"Nathaniel and Lonzo Johnson."

"Where are they from?"

"Detroit."

"Do you have their current address?"

"All I know is they rent a big beige house on Golden Valley Road – I don't know the address. I just know how to get there."

"Alrighty. Thanks for your time Mr. Williams; I'll have the deputy's escort you back to your unit. Here's my card, call me if you have any more details about that night." As they were buzzed out the door, Roberts said, "Damn, you're good." Jones responded in a British accent; "It's elementary my dear Watson, Elementary. Hey, sittin in the county jail, being from a different city, and cold sandwiches for lunch will open a person right up."

"Too bad he couldn't tell us who did it."

"If he'd knew he'd tell. He just minimized his part so he wouldn't get in trouble. I only believe 90 percent of what people I interrogate say. The ones that are trying to stay out of trouble are the one's that tell what everybody else did. Let's send a car to pick up Mr. Johnson and Mr. Sams."

It took several weeks for them to locate Mr. Johnson. L, sat in the City Hall interrogation room, nervously rubbing his hands together. Detective Jones walked in and said, "Hello Mr. Johnson, my name is detective Jones. How's everything going?"

"I'm cool."

"I'm here to talk to you about your friends murder. First, let me say a prayer with you."

"O.k.," he said nervously. After the Lord's prayer, Detective Jones said, "I've been told the details of the fight, so I won't go over that. I want to know who shot Mr. Whitaker."

"I can't really say, it was dark out and it was people everywhere. All I know is Big D was fightin some dude that came off the porch jump Lil' D."

"Where were you when the fight occurred?"

I was standing in front of Big D when he was fightin the dude on the ground, and another one dropkicked him. After that, I heard shots behind me and ran to the car. I wasn't goin to stick around to see who was shootin." Detective Jones showed L a photo lineup of all the people's faces that came up during the investigation and L picked out the person who was fightin Lil D. He thanked L, gave him his card, and told him he'd be in contact with him if he had any more questions.

Later that day, Jones sat in front of his computer staring at Duane Lenway. His rap sheet was full of minor stuff; Jones sat

thinking if he could be the triggerman, he kept an open mind because he saw the most gruesome murders committed by people
who'd never committed a crime in their lives. He placed an APB
on Mr. Lenway and he would talk to him when the time came.
Jones thought, this one will get solved no matter what it takes or
who did or didn't do it. These gang-bangers are killing the city I
grew up in, and I won't stand by and let that happen. He knew,
the more people, the more they had to say, as he leaned back and
took a sip of chamomile. It has been a while since James went
anywhere since the incident over North. All he did was attend to
goals, work, and juggle both Zaria and Lisa. That was hectic at
times, it seemed they both were needy.

He put it in the back of his mind as he watched his car go
through the car wash. He'd saved some money, bought: 15 inch
woofers, a bazooka sub-woofer, tweeters, and a snatch-off Al-
pine C.D. Player; he got a donation from Lisa and painted the car
jet black. It looked good sittin on 18-inch chrome rims.

Now, all he needed was a house to go with the car. He was
on his way. With selling weed he'd purchased from Louie, and
working, he'd have his own place soon. After washing his car, he
headed to Louie's. At Louie's, they sat in the bedroom as Louie
counted the money James gave him to re-up. After James broken
up the ounces, he figured he could make a good return off what
Louie sold him. Louie didn't mind sellin James ounces for cheap.
He knew was a real dude, and always-aided Louie when he needed it, hell, he did it when Louie didn't need it. To show James his
appreciation; he sold him ounces of Rez dro for half price, while
everyone else had to pay full price.

James thanked Louie, went to his car, popped the trunk, and put the four ounces under the carpet behind the side panel, and headed to Lisa's so he could break the ounces down and bag them up. James and Lisa had gotten closer the last few months. She hid his weed for him, or carried it in her bra when they were together, and hid his gun a time or two. Maybe she liked the suspense in helping him. He never asked, as long as she wanted to be Bonnie, he'd be Clyde. Joe would be out in a couple years; James knew Joe was going to have fun with his newfound freedom. So James' plan was to get an apartment, and put Joe some money to the side and pick up where they left off.

It had been two days since Detective Jones put the APB out on Duane Lenway. Duane sat in the interrogation room at City Hall wondering what he was arrested for when Detective Roberts and Jones walked in. "Good afternoon Mr. Lenway. My name is Detective Roberts and this is my partner, Detective Jones. We're here to talk to you about a murder that occurred at a party you attended. Before you say you weren't there. I've already confirmed through a photo line-up that you were fighting Mr. Williams."

"I don't know who that is."

Sifting through his notes, Roberts pulled Lil D's mug shot out and showed it Duane.

"Does this face look familiar?"

"Oh yeah, I remember him."

"Is this the guy you were fighting?"

"Why?"

"You're not in any trouble. I want to know if you and this guy fought, and what it was over."

"I don't have much to say about it."

"Listen, I already know you were just fighting. There are no other allegations or charges."

"So, you're not tryin to charge me with anything?"

"No. I just want to know what happened."

"It's not much to tell.

They tried to get in the party, I told them they couldn't get in and they started talkin shit. At first, James held me back, but, dude kept talkin so I jumped off the porch and swung on him."

"When the shots were fired, where were you?"

"I don't really remember, I was all over the place. Um, James and the fat dude were fightin, and I was fightin him," he said while pointing at the picture of Little D.

"O.k., I see."

"Who's James?"

"I don't really know him. Kev introduced me to him."

"Who is Kev?"

"Oh, they from over South, they came to kick it with us."

"So let me see. It was James and Mr. Whitaker fighting?"

"If that's the fat dude's name, yeah. Other than that, I don't know who did the shootin – it came outta nowhere."

"Alright, Mr. Lenway, have a nice day; here's my card if you have any more information." Detective Roberts and Jones left the interrogation room and headed for their office. Later, they stood looking at a board with: Vino, Fred, Joe, and James on it. They were both thinking the same thing – James Blakely, a South Side Vice Lord. Looks like we might have to pay a visit to Mr. Blakely.

Later that month, James was pulled over, placed in cuffs, and taken to the City Hall interrogation room. As he sat there wondering what was going on, Detectives Roberts and Jones walked in.

"Heeey, long time no see James. I see you're all grown up now, no more peach fuzz. I can't wait to send you to prison. Said Detective Roberts.

James said in an irritated voice, "whatchu want?"

"I want to know why you shot Mr. Whitaker seven times? Was he beatin the shit out of you?"

James sat there trying to recall any recent incidents he'd been in and couldn't think of any; when Detective Roberts showed him a mug shot of Mr. Whitaker, James thought, damn, that's the fat mothafucka that dived on me over North. James looked at both detectives and invoked his right to a lawyer.

"Oh, you wanna be a funny guy? Well, I hope you like laughin in a cell," said Detective Roberts. He opened the door, and motioned for two uniformed police officers to cuff, and take James to be booked for murder.

CHAPTER TWELVE

COUNTY BLUEZ

Five hours later, James stood outside the holding room calling home. Answering the phone, James Sr. said, "Hello."

"Hey dad, what's up? This is me, I'm in the county Jail."

"For what?"

"They say I killed somebody."

In an excited tone his dad said, "What, what the fuck you talkin about, they say you killed somebody?" James had never heard his dad cuss or even raise his voice; he knew this was serious."

"I can't say much on the phone. I'll have to wait until I get a lawyer, so I can figure this all out. Right now, I'm in the booking area, so my time is limited. I'll call you when I can." Remembering all the stuff he went through when he was in prison. James Sr.

told James to be careful and not to talk to anyone, because them nigga's will jump on his case. After James got off the phone, he was told to sit in the holding cell, they called the bullpen. He could see why. He sat there on a concrete slab, trying to ignore the smell of vomit coming off of a man sitting in the middle of the floor mumbling to himself. This is disgusting, he thought. He bent over holding his head in his hands listening to a skinny dark-skinned guy with a dingy white t-shirt, leaning over a stainless steel toilet trying to make himself vomit up drugs he swallowed prior to being arrested. James was so caught up in his thoughts; he didn't have time to be disgusted anymore. He sat there tryin to figure out how he got in this situation. He fought the dude, but he didn't kill him. In fact, he didn't have a gun that night. The more he thought about it, the more he tried to remember who was doing the shootin. It had to be one of them cats from over North, because had it been one of the people with him, he would've known about it. What the fuck, he thought as he heard his last name being called. He was escorted to a dorm with about sixteen guys in it, with four octogen stainless steel tables, and a T.V. mounted in the wall, behind safety glass. He was assigned to a bottom bunk. He unrolled his blanket, made his bed, sat back, and check out the environment. It was strange because he had never been to jail before; for the most part, guys sat around playin spades for candy bars, watchin T.V. or sat in their bunks reading. James noticed a phone on the wall by the bathroom area, he called his dad.

Later that evening, he grabbed a Louis Lamore book, sat back, and read. He couldn't concentrate on the book, he just looked over the top of it to really see who he was in the unit with. Everyone seemed normal, he didn't let his guard down, he recalled what his dad told him about beatin the hell out of the first person who said anything wrong to him, and he was stayin alert to the guys that jump on people's cases. The next morning, James heard his name called over a loud speaker, so he could go to court. He sat and waited on them to come get him> He was handcuffed to a light-skinned guy with a short afro. James didn't pay him much attention, though he noticed a six-pointed star with pitchforks on his forearm. James thought, just my luck. He sat in the bullpen for two hours listening to people swap lies of being rich, all the women they had, and how the state didn't have no case. James was amused by the blatant lies that were going back and forth; he even grinned at a few pimp stories he'd heard. An hour later, he was standing behind plexiglass, separating him from the rest of the courtroom. Some guy, with a brown tweed suit and tight beige khakis approached him and told him he was representing him for arraignment. He barely got to know the guy's name. He disappeared to the other side of the courtroom, talking to some people sittin at a table. James stood there waiting for the fast-talkin somebody to tell him what was goin on. A few minutes later, a courtroom deputy told everyone to rise.

"Hello your honor. I am here representing Mr. Blakely on one count of second degree murder."

"Is there any objection from the state?" asked Judge Robert Martins.

"No your honor."

"In that case, how does your client plead?"

"Not guilty, your honor."

"O.k., we'll set bail at $200,000."

What the fuck? James thought. The geeky looking public defender rushed ove to James and told him he'd see him later. James interrupted and asked why his bail was set so high. The public defender explained to him, that he had to pay ten percent to get out on bail. Later, James sat in the bullpen doing the calculations in his head. He had the ten percent; all he had to do was get to the phone.

James Sr. answered the phone. "Hey, what's up dad?"

In a concerned tone, his dad said "what's goin on? When are they going to arraign you?"

"They already did."

"How come you didn't tell me?"

"I didn't want to bother you with all this mess, and take a day off work to come down here for the monkey show."

"I an make my own decisions, thank you."

"Well, my bail is $200,000, they want ten percent up front, and I can get bailed out."

"I'll have to make a few calls to Gary and talk to Kenny and see what's up."

"Nah, I'm cool. Go to my room, look in the closet, find the shoebox on the bottom left hand side of the closet. I'll call the bail bondsman, talk to him, and you can take him the money."

"Alright."

"I'll call back later." James Sr. hung up the phone and headed to James room, opened the door, and thought, he always keeps his room neat. He found the shoebox, opened it and saw the money. He counted the money and was surprised that James had $47,300. Whatever he's been doin, this is getting his ass outta jail,

he thought as he waited on James to call to see what bails bondsman he had to drop the money off to.

James called three hours later. They called Larson and Larson
bail bonds; the bail bondsman gave them instructions on how to
bring them the money, and they would arrange the bail with the
jail. All James had to do was wait. After he hung up, Michael Larson made a call to a close friend of his. "Hey Jack, this is Mike.
How's the crime rate these days?"

"You know, it's job security. What's up?"

"I just got a call from that fellow you've put word out on."

"Oh yeah, what's he saying?"

"He has the money alright. His dad has the house and bond
in cash. He'll be here tomorrow, he had to get some paper work
out of a safety deposit box on the house."

"Can you stall them?"

"Of course I can. You know my son is having a birthday party; it would be nice if you stopped by for the festivities; a nice
donation to his college fund wouldn't hurt either."

"Hey, you have a friend in my pocket book." Detective Roberts
hung up the phone, headed home, so he could get prepared for
a night on the town. Later that night, Detective Roberts stepped
into Solid Gold gentlemen's club. He spoke to the bouncer, then
asked, if Mr. W was in. He knew he was there, Mr. W was always
there, and he wanted to know who summoned him, so he could
use the back door to cover his indiscretions. While he waited,
he admired the women dancing, or walking around topless. This
was a nice place, it was a little expensive for his pocket book. The
bouncer arrived, escorted Roberts to a private room down some
stairs in another section of the club. Roberts entered and noticed

a caramel-skinned woman with large breasts, and no bottoms on, um, he thought, I wouldn't mind having a little of that. Waiving the nude woman away so Roberts could have some privacy, Roberts said, "What's up Mr. W?"

"Call me Dave."

"I know. I have to mess with you about your code name."

"It's useful. So what brings you to this part of town Jack?" and handed him a shot of Jack Daniels with no ice.

Taking a sip. "Woo, this is nice."

"It's from my private stock."

"Whelp, I have a situation. You remember that Robinson case a few years back?"

"Yeah, I signed a couple warrants for you on that case."

"I have one of the guys responsible under the clock."

"I have him on another one, but I think if I can hold him a little longer, I can get him to talk."

"What do I have to do with this?"

"He talked to Mike, and he has the 200 and the property."

"I see. Whelp, Jack, quid pro quo, quid pro quo. I have an election coming up, and my foundation is in need of some serious charitable contributions."

Holding his hand up, Detective Roberts said, "say no more. I'll be at the dinner, and you got my vote." They shook hands; Roberts swallowed his last shot of brandy, and left the club with a smile on his face. He had one more call to make.

Two days later, James sat wondering why he was in court. He didn't have a hearing until next month. While he sat wondering what was up, he heard the bailiff tell everyone to rise for Judge

David Weinberg. The public defender representing James said, "Good morning your honor."

"Good morning counsel."

"Your honor, my client is wondering why we are here. I'm stumped as well."

"I know this is short notice, but we're here to discuss a motion that came to me in the middle of the evening – I'll let the state explain it."

"Good morning your honor. We're here to motion the court to modify Mr. Blakely's bail. We would like your honor to raise it."

"Objection your honor, what-"

"Over-ruled. Counsel, you may continue."

"Mr. Blakely has been implicated in other murders, we believe he is a flight risk, and that witnesses may be intimidated and compelled not to testify in this case, due to Mr. Blakely's association with the vice lords gang your honor."

"O.k., I'll grant the motion, and set bail at 2 million. Good day everyone." Judge Weinberg left the courtroom. James sat there thinking how he was going to come up with 2 million dollars. All he had was the twenty thousand for the first bond.

As he left the courtroom, he thought, I couldn't believe this shit.

Later that evening, James called his dad to let him know what was up. His dad's reaction was less than subtle. He hurled insults at the prosecutor and judge; he reminded James of how vicious white folks are when they want to pin a black man to the cross. James listened with no emotion, and let his dad talk for 15 minutes, until the call was over.

After the call, James laid back on his bunk and re-read his charge papers, thinking, how crazy this shit is. The next morning, James sat on his bunk thinking about his situation, when a medium height skinny guy who wore circular metal rimmed glasses, they called slim approached him with a newspaper.

"They gotchu in the paper ride."

James looked at the photo of himself, the headline read: LOCAL MAN ARRESTED IN KILLING OF DETROIT NATIVE. He continued to read the article, it stated he killed Donald Whitaker, 23, while in a fight at a party and bail was set at 2 million dollars. James stared at the article in disbelief. He gave the paper back, and headed for the phone to call Zaria.

That evening, James sat on his bunk laying back, when he heard the Cuban trustee loudly talking to a white guy half his size in bad English. He watched intently, because he knew the conversation was more than an argument. The short white guy threw the first punch. The trustee stumbled backward, and fell against a table where a few guys were gambling. The white guy followed up with consecutive punches to his face, blood spurted from a cut above the trustee's eye. The trustee screamed, said something in Spanish, got his footing, and rushed the white guy with his six foot, two hundred pound frame into a metal rail that supported the bunk bed.

His body seemed to wrap around the rail of the bunk bed; he hit the floor with a thud. The trustee bent at the waist, and placed blows to the white guys face until the deputies rushed in the unit and broke up the fight. James laid back down after the deputy's left. He thought, the white boy had him, he shouldn't have let up. I know for certain, the first person who says anything to me, justice will be served.

Three days later, James sat in front of a public defender named David Crumwell. He listened intently to what he had to say. James thought, this guy is a quack. How can he go to trial with the shit he's talkin about. I need a real lawyer. James asked a few questions, and listened for the scripted answers, thanked him, and left.

That evening James was talkin to his dad about using the bail money for a lawyer. He reminded him to eat on the other money, and let him take care of the rest. The next day James Sr. was on the phone with an old friend from Gary.

"Yello."

"You still answer the phone the same. Boy, you'll never change."

"Is this J-Lord?"

"Yeah, it's me Skippy."

In an excited voice, Skippy said "Oh shit bruh, I haven't heard form you in awhile. What's up? I thought you retired chief?"

"I am. I'm going through some stuff with my son, James."

"What's up with Lil' James bruh?"

"He's wrapped up in a murder."

"What? Whatchu need me to do chief?"

"I'll let you know when I hit the city; I was just callin to let you know I'm on my way."

"I'm at a new spot. When you get in town, come to the Gentlemen's Palace, right off 5th Avenue."

"I'm on my way." James hung up the phone and stared at the books on the shelf in his office. He thought, he'd never have to use this phone book again. He said, out loud to himself, "I guess ol' J-Lord is back. The next day, James talked to his supervisor, took a two-week vacation – that night he was on 94 east non-stop to Gary.

Four and a half hours later, he was layin back in a hotel room thinking about his next move, first he had to go see Skippy. "Heey chief, what's goin on? You look good bruh."

"Thanks Skip. You don't look too shabby yourself." Looking around the strip club, "I see you got a nice little situation here."

"Yeah, I had to put the pistol down, and get my head in a different game. Yeah bruh, welcome to the Gentleman's Palace. Come on, let me get you a drink, a dance, and something for you to take to the hoe-tel."

"Nah, I'm here on business bruh;" waiving James to follow him to his office downstairs, they sat and James told him about the situation with his son. Skip's response was "Say no more." Two hours later, James opened a large duffle bag and counted $150,000. Looks good to me bruh. You know I'd love to stay and holla atcha, but I gotta get on the road in the morning." As James turned to leave, Skip said, "Hey chief, you see what I got goin on, if you need more, let me know."

"This will do for now," said James as he headed out the door into the cool night. James took the bag, and placed it in the trunk, got in the dark blue 1989 ninety-eight Oldsmobile, took three no-doze caffeine tablets, and headed o 94 West so Amy McCarther could get the money she needed to represent his son. As he pushed down on the gas, he though, fuck that hotel, I gotta take care of some business.

James stood in line to go to the gym so he could lift some weights, and stretch his legs. As the deputies escorted them, they stopped in front of a unit, so the deputy could drop some papers off. James stood there wondering why this light-skinned skinny guy was yelling at him through the glass; James focused on his mouth, he could read his lips sayin "you killed my nigga, it's on when I see you." It hit James. Ooh, that's the mothafucka from the party over North.

James wasn't concerned because he didn't kill anybody, and it was highly unlikely that that chump would do anything through the thick glass. He focused his attention on his surroundings, waited for the deputy to finish his business and headed to the gym. Three days later, James was called for a lawyer visit.

He entered the room, and shook hands with a petite white woman with dark blue eyes and dark brown hair that was pulled back into a bun, wearing a black pants suit that showed her curves. She looked at James wide-eyes, shook his hand, and said "My name is Amy McCarther, your dad hired me to represent you in this case." They sat down, she gave James an extensive background about her career as an attorney. Her first mission was to get a bail reduction, then she'd proceed to get the case in front of another judge because Judge Weinberg wasn't called hang em high for nothin. James sat and listened intently and asked questions he felt were important; he was satisfied with the answers, and relaxed a little.

An hour later, they shook hands and he was escorted back to the unit. Two weeks later, James heard a deputy call his name to roll up his bunk because he was being moved to another unit. The unit he was in was reserved for non-murder cases. Everyone with murder cases were placed in a unit together, due to the severity of their crime. James rolled his stuff up, said his goodbyes, and made his way to the other unit.

He walked in the unit and noticed the surroundings were a little better, he had a single cell, which meant more privacy and the unit had windows that allowed him to see parts of downtown Minneapolis. The view wasn't that great because the windows were filthy, but James could see the tops of cars and people's heads as they passed by. As James stood there looking at the sky, he listened to some older guys play a quiet game of dominoes.

He noticed a few guys in front of a cell doing push ups – the unit seemed laid back, there were less than twenty people, that was a plus and if it got too loud, he could shut the door. James heard one of the older guys playin dominoes say, "What up D, you wanna get your head split next?"

"Nah, old man, you remember what I did to you yesterday." James looked over his shoulder to see who the extra voice was, and locked eyes with Lil' D, who threatened him a few weeks ago. Instantly, James though this was the unit, but it was empty when he came in, so he must've been in his cell. James didn't waste time. He kicked his slippers off, and rushed in Lil D's direction, as fast as his bare feet would carry him. Surprised, Lil D jumped up from the stool and tried to stand his ground. He was too late and too slow, James met his slow reaction with a blow to his eye, instantly Lil D tried to grab James around the waist. James slung Lil D into the wall, as Lil D hit the wall, and slid to the floor; James hit him with a fury of blows that could be heard with every land to his face and head. "Alright, alright, I'm done," Said Lil D through the blood pouring from his mouth.

"Do it now, do it now!" Screamed James. One of the older men playing dominoes walked over to James and said in a calm voice, "Hey young blood, cool out, you don't want to catch another case, you gone kill him." James threw a few more punches to Lil D's head, and sat on the stool at the table. The older man helped Lil D off the floor, and escorted him to his cell.

James sat there, watchin Lil D cup his hands over his mouth and nose in an attempt to stop the blood from spurting out his face. The more he watched Lil D, the more he thought about his situation and the shit Lil D started that night. James got up, ran over Lil D before he made it to his cell, and threw a two piece combination to the tip of his chin; Lil D hit the floor with a thud. James stood over him waitin for him to move. He looked down at his body, grinned, and went to his cell to was Lil D's blood off his hands.

Two days later Lil D laid in a cell thinkin about what happened. He wanted to get James back, but he couldn't. He didn't have the fightin skills, and the time he was facin, it was highly probably that he wouldn't have access to a gun for the next thirty years. He laid there, eased out of bed, and went to the phone. He leaned against the wall to hold himself up, it felt like his ribs were broken – the phone range on the other end, just as Lil D started to hang up, he heard Detective Roberts' voice on the other end. James sat in the visiting booth talking to his dad, getting an update on what was going on with the family. It was the usual, but different because he wasn't there. He talked about his last few visits with Amy, she sounded like she was going to get him out of this situation.

The forensics reports weren't in line with James lying on the ground while the victim was standing. There were no eyewitnesses; in fact, the witnesses they had said James didn't shoot. And the shots came from behind James. She was shocked that they didn't drop the case. In the back of James' mind, he knew the detectives were tryin to put him in a tight spot so they could squeeze him on the Damian Roberts murder – he wasn't budging. Two months later, James sat down diligently listening to Amy scold him.

"Why'd you tell this guy this stuff, then you beat the shit out of him. They have pictures of his face, James. I'm trying to get you outta prison, not put you in one. James stared at the statement from Devon Williams aka Little D. He called the detectives and told them, James assaulted him to keep him quiet about him seeing James shoot Big D the night of the party. He couldn't believe what he was reading. He told Amy why he fought Lil D. She understood, and pointed out to him Lil D's prior statement about him runnin and not seeing who did the shooting; she'd get it throw out at an upcoming hearing. That night, James laid back in his bunk thinkin about how he wished he could give Lil D a bath with some .38 slugs.

Chapter Thirteen

Hang Em' High

J ames leaned back in his seat wearing black slacks, white shirt, black tie, while his dark black blazer hung over the back of the chair. He listened intently as Amy asked potential jurors about their past, likes, dislikes, or if they had been a victim of a violent crime. They had been there almost two weeks, and had picked eight jurors; all the other potential choices were struck down by the prosecutor. Amy objected, because it seemed that, if any jurors that were young, black, or were from the North Side of Minneapolis, they were struck from the panel. Judge Weinberg, over ruled her objections, and allowed the State to strike the jurors. James could see why they called him Hang Em' High. Voir dire lasted all day.. By the time jury selection ended, and James made it back to the unit, he slept until the next morning.

By the end of that month, they had a jury. It wasn't one to Amy's liking, but with Weinberg's hard on for James she did the best she could. The States' witness list wasn't impressive. She was sure Mr. William's testimony wouldn't be allowed. It was clear that he made it up because James beat him up for making threats. The first motion to suppress his testimony was denied; she'd submit another one before he came to testify. And, she was definitely going to Spiegel him. He had a track record of carjacking, robbery, assaults in Detroit, now he was in Minnesota locked up on a murder with two eyewitnesses. She leaned back and listened to Duane Lenway testify to not seeing anything. Once the State was done questioning him, Amy stood up and said, " Mr. Lenway, did you see Mr. Blakely shoot Mr. Whitaker?"

"No."

" So, it is your testimony that you did not see Mr. Blakely with a gun or shoot a gun on the night of the incident?"

"Yes."

" It is also your testimony that Mr. Blakely was lying on the ground being assaulted by Mr. Whitaker?"

"Yes." She stood there with her arms crossed. "No more questions."

The rest of the day was about questioning the coroner, and Amy arguing about not letting the jurors see the photos of the dead body of Mr. Whitaker, which was denied by Judge Weinberger. James was escorted by a deputy back to the unit; he sat back and thought about the judge. He couldn't figure out why he wasn't lettin his attorney do what she needed to do to get him acquitted; they knew he didn't do it, he couldn't figure it out, so he laid back and went to sleep.

The next day, he entered the courtroom and saw Zaria in the front row with his

Family, and Lisa sat two rows behind them. He didn't acknowledge anyone, he didn't want Zaria and Lisa to bump heads; that was the last thing he needed. He leaned back and watched the jury come in, and stood when Judge Weinberg took his seat. Amy waited until the State questioned the forensics expert, Janice Gulgowski. When they were done, Amy sat there for a second pretending to be in deep thought.

She looked at Ms. Gulgowski and said, " So the bullet wounds were inconsistent with a person firing from the ground?"

"Yes."

"That would mean, the bullet's came from behind the person lying on the ground?"

"Yes."

"Is it possible for a person lying on the ground to make those types of wounds if they fired a gun?"

"No."

"So, you're saying the person on the ground did not shoot a gun?"

"Yes."

James sat there, hoping the judge would recognize that there is no possible way for him to shoot a gun from the position he was in. The judge just leaned back in his black leather chair, and acted as if he didn't hear the testimony. The next few days were intense. Amy submitted a motion to dismiss the case with prejudice. The evidence thus far, didn't stand up to the standards of a guilty verdict, nor was it enough to charge James with murder. It was denied, as if she sent Judge Weinberg a joke on paper. They rested for three weeks because the judge had a vacation, and he didn't want the case to be handed to another judge.

Three weeks later, Detective Roberts sat on the stand telling his version of the investigation. Since he was a veteran officer that had testified in many trials, he knew how to avoid questions, and testify as if the person on trial were in fact guilty of the crime. The thing that got James was, when Roberts accidentally told the court that he investigated a murder James was involved in prior to the one he was charged with.

James' lawyer screamed, "objection!" and demanded that his comment be stricken from the record, and that the jury be dismissed, to given a curative instruction regarding his so-called slip of the tongue. James leaned back in his chair, and stared at Detective Roberts and grinned at him in his cheap suit. Detective Roberts sat there trying to look as if he didn't do anything wrong; his attempt to make James look guilty in the eyes of the jurors didn't phase him. He went through all the trouble to attend Judge Weinberg's $10,000 a plate dinner for his foundation at for the Children's Hospital, as well as, the money he had to give to stall them on the bail; he was going to let the jurors know James was involved in another murder- that was for damn sure. If it worked, it would be a notch in his belt, if it didn't, he'd stay on James' ass until his career ended. The judge gave the court reporter permission to strike the comment from the record, and told the jurors to ignore what they'd heard.

Amy continued questioning Roberts about the case, she asked Judge Weinberg to make him give a yes or no answer if he had any evidence that James had shot Mr. Whitaker. The judge with all his conspiratorial might overruled her request. Amy figured she'd cover it in her closing argument. All the witnesses that day agreed that James wasn't the shooter, but a victim of an assault. Two days later, Devon Williams sat on the stand with a dark blue blazer, tan shirt, blue tie, and matching slacks. The prosecutors paid to get him looking the best they could because he was the key to their case, as long as he stuck to his statement, that he saw James kill Big 0, it was a definite conviction. Lil' D, sat there trying to look as if he'd never committed a dozen crimes in his life. The prosecutor in all his mischievousness laid the icing on the cake at the out-set of questioning Lil' D. "Mr. Williams, who killed your best friend Mr. Whitaker?"

Pointing at James through teary eyes he said, "he did."

"No more questions."

Amy questioned Lil' D with so much zeal and anger, that he stuttered the entire time she questioned him. It was obvious he was lying. But, the judge let him continue with his tirade of lies. When she asked him about the initial statement he gave, the prosecutor objected. Judge Weinberg called them to the bench. As they sat there discussing whether or not her line of questioning was proper, Lil' D sat there trying to ignore James' stare. He leaned back in the chair rubbing the superficial wound to his leg; he received the night Big D was killed. Even though he knew he accidently killed Big D, and accidently shot himself pulling the gun from his pants pocket; he didn't care, because had James not came off the porch and jumped in his business he wouldn't be in this situation. He was shootin at James anyway, had Big D not stood up, he'd still be alive.

Lil' D was surprised no one saw him fire the shots. It was probably because everyone was too busy fighting or runnin when they heard the shots. They must've saw him run in the direction of the house, and thought he was runnin from the fight. It didn't matter, as long as he wasn't being charged with anything; he'd had enough problems in his life. And James breaking his jaw was his way of puttin the nails in his coffin. Amy came back to the table, and let James know that, the judge wouldn't allow her to question Lil' D about his first statement. James shook his head, letting her know he understood what she was saying. Amy questioned Lil' D some more trying to get him to admit that he was intentionally lying on James. Her efforts were to no avail. She kept on questioning him until the judge told her it was enough, it had been a half-hour, and he was getting tired of her asking the same question inn different forms.

Lil D finished his testimony, got off the stand, and was escorted back to his unit. James sat there hoping he would run into Lil' D. He sighed, leaned back, and wondered what was next. The next day, the State did its closing argument. They tried convincing the jury that James shot and somehow slid under Big D, that was the most preposterous thing James had heard in his life. He kept thinking, how do you shoot someone seven times , and then slide underneath them? The jury has to know this is a joke.

Amy gave her closing argument with the fact that, the forensics expert said he couldn't have shot him lying on the ground, the coroner testified that, the bullet wounds were received as a result of Big D standing up, and Lil' D was an outright liar who was testifying to get even with James. The trial concluded, the judge gave the jurors their instructions, and not the cautionary instruction Amy requested. The jurors left to deliberate the case, now James' fate was in their hands. For three days James sat in the unit wondering what the jurors were thinking.

On the fourth day, he was called to the courtroom because the jurors returned a verdict. James sat next to Amy while she held his hand. The jurors were seated, and the verdict was a unanimous guilty of one count of second-degree murder. Amy squeezed James' hand so tight; he thought she was trying to break his fingers. Amy quickly polled the jury to no avail. The judge dismissed the jury so he could sentence James. Amy objected because there was no presentence investigation done, and this was James' first time being incarcerated – Judge Weinberg told Amy to sit down, or he would have her removed from his courtroom.

He asked James to stand before the court, James stayed in his seat staring at the judge with his head held high. and said, " Do whatever it is you're going to do."

"In that case, I sentence you to the statutory maximum of forty years."

Amy jumped from her seat, and yelled, "Objection your honor; the maximum penalty is 200 months, you're exceeding the guidelines by at least 22 years."

"This is my court room. if you don't like it, appeal it to another court; as it stands, 400 months is the maximum, and that is the sentence I am passing down. Good day counsel." James sat there thinking, this dude is a real clown, as they escorted him out of the courtroom, and back to the unit. Amy told James she'd appeal his case and come see him as soon as possible. He acknowledged what she said, and thought about his future. At the unit, James changed clothes and went to his cell to await the next phase of this bad dream. He wondered if his conviction was because of the wrongs he did in the past. Whatever it was, he had to hold his head high, the last thing he wanted to do was break under pressure.

Later that evening, Amy came to visit James. She told him she would do his appeal, and it would be for free. She saw what they had done to him, and she was sorry and disgusted. And, no matter what she'd get him out of prison. Somehow, she'd have to get Moony to look into what was going on behind the scenes.

Before James left, she gave him a hug and tears welled in her eyes, she had grown fond of James while she was representing him. She had represented plenty of people between Minnesota and New York, but James was different - she couldn't figure where the intimate feelings came from, she didn't know of it was his smile, his laid back disposition, whatever it was, she wanted more of it. Her plans to take James out to dinner after his trial were interrupted by Judge Weinberg, and she would see to it that Judge Weinberg would regret what he did.

Four days later, James was in the back of the Sherriff's dark brown Chevy Suburban, sittin in shackles and waist chains on his way to prison. The Suburban pulled up to the prison, it reminded James of a castle with its tall walls, and gothic architecture. He managed to walk the best he could with shackles on. A few minutes after he entered the front door, he sat there waiting to be escorted to a cell hall.

James was housed in B-House on the second galley. He was quarantined for 24 hours, until he was cleared by the doctor that he didn't have any infectious diseases. It was the prison routine, so he kicked back thinking about what had just been done to him. He hadn't the time to ponder on the judge's scheme earlier, because he had visits and everyone wanted him to call before he was transferred to prison. As he dozed into a fitful sleep, he thought how cold the game is when the devils don't play fair.

The next day, he was escorted to the medical unit where he was given a full medical

Screening. He was cleared of having any infectious diseases, and was taken back to the unit. Once he got back to the unit he had the chance to review his environment. it was a cell house with about 200 people or less in it, with several phones, a shower area, a small laundry room, and a few T.V.'s mounted to the walls, along with two vending machines. For the most part, it was a different world, before James headed to the phone to call his dad, he told himself, the first time someone says anything out of pocket, I'm going to teach em' a grave lesson. He talked to his dad for 15 minutes, and established visits, and a schedule to stay in contact with his family after they were off work. After he got a visiting and phone schedule together, he spent the rest of the day sittin in his cell listenin' to the voices and soounds of B-House.

CHAPTER FOURTEEN

B-HOUSE

J ames woke the next morning, and made his way to breakfast. it wasn't anything special, he kept his head down and ate, purposely ignoring the feeling that he was being watched. Forty minutes later, he was on his way up the stairs to his cell when he was approached by a tall heavy-set guy who introduced himself as Prince. Prince asked James where he was from. James gave him a short bio, and Prince let him know he was vice lord from the West Side of Chicago. Prince introduced James to the other Brotha's in the unit, they were sittin at a table playin cards and watchin T.V..

James sat and talked to Prince who called it for B-House for the Brotha's, he gave him all the do's and don'ts of the unit. He explained to him about security on the showers, where they ate in the chow hall, and how to deal with any problems that may arise while they were in the unit together. He also reminded James that the unit they were in was an intake unit so; he wouldn't be there long.

Prince was a long term resident because he was the unit swamper. James was given all the necessities he needed until he went to canteen. He wasn't worried about a T.V., he'd get that when his dad sent it. In the meantime, he took in the dull scenery and unusual vibe of the unit. Though, he was with the Brotha's, he was still on his P's and Q's. Later that night, James was sittin talkin to Prince and saw his first fight in a prison setting. It wasn't anything special, just two white guys scrappin over something James had nothin to do with.

After the squad came and broke up the fight, and escorted them to seg. Prince said. "See James, if them white boys ever get outta pocket, we crushin em' bruh. Raising his voice. Prince said, " It's west Side till I die in this bitch."

"Yeah I hear ya bruh."

"You gotta remember them white boys runnin around without shit on they chest tryin to flex and shit; fuck them ho's. Wanna be Nazi bitches."

"What shit of ours do they have on their chest?"

"That swastika. Bruh, they stole the grammadon and tilted it, now they call it a swastika. I'm up on them ho's, and how they steal and take our African thoughts, ideas, works, and twist em'."

"Hmmm, I didn't know that."

"Yeah bruh, while you're here studying the prophet's teachings and study the law, or you'll leave this place dumb as a box of rocks, fuckin with these slow ass nigga's in here." James sat and thought about what Prince told him.

"Who's the prophet?"

"Noble Drew Ali bruh. These Negroes adopt the Sunni Islam script. Me, I honor the prophet. He teaches us about our culture, heritage, and the Islam that was passed down to us by our fore-fathers, not the white-Arabs. You gotta be on your toes, or you'll get swallowed up in this cesspool of stupidity."

James sat there listening to Prince talk about all the things he learned at the Moorish Science Temple; it was cool, but James was interested in the law. That was his mission. "What's up with the law you were talkin about.?"

"I'll take you up there tomorrow, and show you how to do re-search, so you can know how to do legal research and understand how the law works." The rest of the night, James sat and talked to Prince. He had a lot of information, he just acted wild and crazy. After James took his shower, he called home, went to his cell, and did some thinking until he fell asleep.

The next morning, he went to breakfast. Since he didn't have a job assigned to him, he sat in his cell listening to people play cards, and watching the T.V.'s on the flag. While he was sittin there, Prince came to his cell." You ready Lord?"

" For what bruh?"

"The law library."

"Oh, yeah." James got his tablet, pencil, and headed to the library with Prince. When he got there, he noticed it was inside the regular library - he expected something a bit bigger.

"Why is this so small?"

"Don't worry bruh; we have all we need. Once, I show you how this demo works you'll be alright." Prince grabbed a book titled, Wests Digest. " This is the book you start with. All research questions start here, in the digest system. It's divided into volumes so you can pin point your issue. O.k., what's your issue?"

"My lawyer told me the judge gave me too much time."

"O.k., sounds like he departed from the sentence."

James sat and watched as Prince guided him through the volumes of books, and it lead him to what he was looking for. James read that the judge couldn't depart from the sentencing guidelines unless he has aggravating factors. James knew none of the rules he read weren't followed, not even a little bit. Prince showed James the Blacks Law dictionary, the Supreme Court Reporters, and the North Western Reporters to look up the cases in Minnesota. James couldn't believe Prince knew how to navigate through this law library like this. They sat and gathered some information on sentencing departures, got copies, and went back to B-House.

Legal research was easier than James thought. For the next month, he attended the law library every day; he had an insatiable thirst for learning and researching the law. Once he memorized the stuff about sentencing, he placed a call to Amy. Amy pushed the button to accept James' call with enthusiasm.

"Hello James."

"Hey, what's up Amy?"

"How come you haven't responded to my letters, and you refused my visit, what's up? You o.k."

"I'm cool. I'm just tryin to wrap this situation around my mind, so I don't berserk."

"Well, I'm here if you need me."

"I called to ask a few questions about the judge departing from the sentencing guidelines."

"Yeah, he can't do that. That's what I wanted to talk to you about. Essentially, the statutory maximum is 40 years, which you couldn't have gotten unless you had at least six criminal history points. I think he did it to be a rotten apple."

James sat there listening to Amy and he understood everything she said. All the studying he did was repeated by Amy, it was as if she was in the law library with him. While she was talking, his mind shifted to the hug she gave him on the day of the conviction. He didn't know if he should ask her, or if it was just an emotional moment- he opted to erase it from his mind.

They ended the conversation with a date that she would come to see him, so she could discuss his appeal. A week later, James was given a job in the kitchen so he was moved to C-House; they called it the gladiators unit because it was always fighting in that unit. It didn't matter to James, he was good with his hands, and he didn't care too much for bullshit. He found his niche in staying in the law library, and if anybody messed that up for even a second, he would be hot on their heels.

CHAPTER FIFTEEN

GLADIATOR SCHOOL

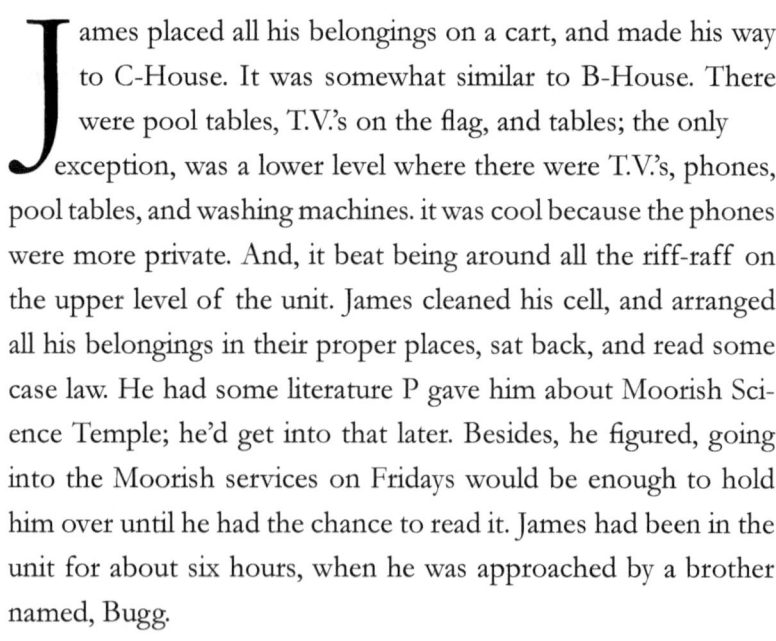

James placed all his belongings on a cart, and made his way to C-House. It was somewhat similar to B-House. There were pool tables, T.V.'s on the flag, and tables; the only exception, was a lower level where there were T.V.'s, phones, pool tables, and washing machines. it was cool because the phones were more private. And, it beat being around all the riff-raff on the upper level of the unit. James cleaned his cell, and arranged all his belongings in their proper places, sat back, and read some case law. He had some literature P gave him about Moorish Science Temple; he'd get into that later. Besides, he figured, going into the Moorish services on Fridays would be enough to hold him over until he had the chance to read it. James had been in the unit for about six hours, when he was approached by a brother named, Bugg.

James saw why he got that name. Bugg was all of 6 foot 6, dark-skinned, skinny with big bugged eyes that looked as if they were protruding out of his head. Prince had told him to get in tune with Bugg when he made it to C-House. Bugg stood in front of James' cell with his palms held high, and greeted him." Lah via va va brotha, my name is Bugg."

James sat up. "Hey brotha, my name is James."

"I ran across Prince a few minutes ago, and he told me you were coming over here. And, that you were a knowledgeable brotha."

"I try to be."

"Well, this is it; there's always something with these studs over here. I can't call it though. it's a lot of Brotha's over here, we stay to ourselves, so we don't have to get involved in the madness, but, if it goes down, we'll be on top of it."

"I hear that, I stay into the law, so my head is between a book or ignoring non-sense."

"That's cool. We need brotha's like you around, so the fold is less volatile. Did they give you your kitchen gear yet?"

"Nah."

"You'll probably get it tomorrow. You'll like the kitchen. You get the chance to eat good, and see all the people in the joint- not that they matter; it's Bugg leaned back to look at the clock. Their finna do count in a minute, so I'll rotate with you when we come out."

"Alright. Mighty."

James sat back and read some case law about sentencing. He had another stack of material on prosecutorial misconduct, and abuse of judicial discretion. He had a plan for Mr. Hang Em High.

Later, James stood on the flag greeting all the Brotha's in the unit. He was also introduced to the Latin Kings, and the Stones. Though, they were from different organizations, they all represented Al-Mighty, so wherever anything happened, it was fin-ball rollin. James was cool with that. Though, they got down together, each mob handled their own internal problems, which made things easier and kept down friction between brotha's.

Bugg pointed out all the different gangs, and groups in the unit. It was different, because James had never been in the same space with Crips, Bloods, Gangsta's, Nazi's, and the Natives in one place without a bunch of tension. It seemed they had their parameters worked out- One thing was for certain, if one black got into it with anyone that wasn't black, all the blacks rolled together.

It was an interesting puzzle James thought. But, he was more interested in reading the case law, that was waiting for him in his cell. After his conversation with Bugg, he made his way to the phone.

"Hello."

"Hey, what's up girl?"

"Ohh, hey babe, I've been waitin on you to call."

" What's the routine?"

"Cards, sports, and dumb shit."

"I can understand that."

"So, when you comin to see me?'

"I'll definitely be there this weekend."

"O.k., that's a plan. I'll definitely be waitin."

For 15 minutes James and Zaria talked about absolutely nothing in James' mind. He felt she seemed distant, and acted as if she were preoccupied. At the end of the day, he didn't care because his mind was on one thing, and it was in his cell lying on the desk. James said his goodbyes, went to his cell, sat and read for the rest of the night. The next day, he was called to report to the kitchen.

He walked to the kitchen, got his white kitchen uniform, and was given his assignment of spraying the trays before they were placed into the washer. It reminded him of the bus boy job he had. It was as easy as apple pie. He stood there sprayin the trays, and checkin out the people who he worked with in the kitchen.

They seemed alright. The brotha's were down there. James paid particular attention to them because they were the loosest people to him. Lorenzo was cool, he didn't talk too much, he had an observant attitude. Lil' Maser on the other hand, was a mess; he was full of energy, every other word out of his mouth was, " I'm C.V.L. crazy."

Big Eric was an embodiment of his name- light-skinned 6 foot 6 and ripped. All he did was lift weights, if you wanted to talk to him; you had to go to the weight pile. Wayne Mo, he was cool. James learned that all the Blackstone's used a suffix at the end of their names to identify that they were one of the Stones. Another thing they had in common, were the cornrows straight to the back. Wayne Mo was about 40. He was short and had a potbelly, before he started a sentence, he would say: " listen here Charlie"

James thought that was funny. All in all, they were brotha's, so he gave them the benefit of the doubt. Later that night, while James was on the phone talking to Lisa, he heard the screech of tennis shoes, when he turned to look, and saw two Native guys fighting. He continued his conversation. It was more wrestling than anything, until the shorter Native threw an over hand right to the other guys nose, and blood spurted from his face. They fought for about two minutes, until the squad came running in, tackling them both to the floor. James shook his head, and continued listening to Lisa use a vibrator she bought to keep her company.

James had been in C-House for about a month, then decided to start going to the Temple to see what Prince was telling him. He found the literature interesting. The thing that stuck out to him was that they used the same principles as the vice lords. Once James figured out that the Moorish Science Temple had been around since the 1930's, he knew love, truth, peace, freedom, and justice was something borrowed. He sat in the front row of the small room, they labeled the chapel, and listened to Dwanyne-Bey give a lesson on why the nationality of the Moors were taken from them.

To his surprise, he found the Moors were punished for violating Allah's laws and as a result, slavery was the penalty for Moors failing to practice the five principles. And, that Allah would assist those who reclaimed their national origin, and up-hold the spiritual principles. He went on for about an hour detailing the differences between.

Moors, Negroes, coloreds, and blacks. James sat wide-eyed. he knew he needed to know more about Moorish Science. After the meeting, he was introduced to more brotha's that came from other units to meet and greet each other, or to discuss whatever business they had to discuss.

Prince and James sat and talked for ten minutes. They had before the chapel closed. He and Prince shook hands, and he made his way back to the unit to read case law that was waiting for him. That Saturday, James went to work, talked on the phone. Later in the day, he came out of his cell to wash his clothes, when he heard an argument at one of the card tables. He didn't have to look because he heard," Listen hear Charlie; you renigged, so that's double bubble."

"Nah, nigga. I ain't done shit."

"Listen here Charlie, you renigged and that's that, you gone pay me my shit."

"Nigga, I ain't payin you shit."

Wayne Mo let his fists finish the rest of the conversation. As Wayne Mo was fighting, James dropped his laundry bag, ran to the fight, and started landing hard blows to the other guy's head. He must've thought he was going to fight one on one; James punched that notion out of his mind, as the guy dropped to the ground and covered his head from the blows. As James reached back to to land a blow to his ribs, he was tackled to the floor, escorted to seg, stripped searched, and placed in a cell. he sat there wishing he had more time, so he could've broke the guys ribs.

He didn't see the hearing officer until Monday; so he sat back and listened to all the guys talking, yelling or arguing. Out of all the voices, he heard Wayne Mo- " Listen here Charlie, me and the young Lord beat that nigga down."

James sat back grinnin, thinkin, that old man is crazy, and shifted his thought to the case law he remembered. Three days later, James signed for 30 days in seg for fighting, it didn't matter to him, because he could get his legal material sand have more sent from the law library.

James was pacing in his cell talking to himself when he was interrupted by a guard doing his round. "You alright?"

Looking confused. James said, "Huh?"

"You're talking to yourself; you o.k.?"

"Ah nah, I was reciting this case law, that's all."

"O.k., if you need to talk to somebody, let me know."

"I'm cool, thanks though." Damn, I wasn't aware that I was doin that shit, thought James. For the next two hours, James walked back and forth mumbling to himself about how the judge abused his discretion.

Three weeks had gone by, as James sat there reading case law. A guard came to his cell and told him he had a legal visit. James prepared the legal documents he wanted to take with him. Since he was in seg, he was handcuffed and escorted to the visiting room.

He sat across from Amy enjoying her smile. She was usual Amy, wearing a suit outfit, with the exception of a short skirt. James noticed the pinned striped skirt exposed some of her thigh, and hugged her curves. Her blouse was opened three buttons down exposing that she didn't have a bra on. James thought it was because he was locked up, that she looked so damn good. He sat there in waist chains, listening to her talk about the issues she would put in his brief for his upcoming appeal.

James listened intently, and tried to ignore the sweet smell of Amy's perfume. They sat and discussed his appeal for two hours, she told him she would send him a copy after she had finished it, and have it filed with the court of appeals. James sat in his cell after the visit, remembering the smell of Amy's perfume, her erect nipples, that peeked through the fabric of her silk blouse, and how her thighs peeked underneath her skirt.

An hour later, he was pacing, having a mock argument with the court of appeals regarding the judges abuse of discretion. James had been out of seg for about a month, when he was in the law library talking to Prince about how to locate information on writing a brief. It seemed to Prince, that James had everything in order; all he needed was the format. He'd noticed since he turned James on to the law, that he was in the law library every day, and every time he saw James, he wouldn't talk about anything else. Prince thought, boy, brotha is for real about this law shit.

As they sat their looking up info on the format of a brief, James asked Prince about the white dude that was always in the law library when they were there. " Maaan, dude ain't white, he's Mexican. That's crazy ass Gomez; that mothafucka crazy as hell bruh."

"Oh yeah?"

"He's not clinically crazy, he's just into that conspiracy theory shit about the government using his name and some other shit."

"For real?"

"Straight up bruh, I don't fuck wit em'."

"I see him in the unit. He stays to him self."

"They say he got one of them cases, that's why people leave his ass alone."

"What case you talkin about?"

"Rumor has it, that he's a homo or rapist, some shit like that."

James looked over at Gomez sittin at the table reading and writing. "Hmm, ain't that something." James went back to what he was doin.

Friday came around, and James was in the front row at the Moorish Science Temple meeting. He had purchased a Moorish Koran; the brotha's called it the Circle Seven, because the cover of the Koran had a circle broken in four sections enclosing the number seven. it was a lot of information, James enjoyed it. He liked the fact, that it was something that taught him about himself.

Though, his dad taught him a lot about black history growing up. Noble Drew Ali's teachings, seemed like a natural transition for him. He sat there listening to Dwayne Bey give a lesson on the difference between Moors and Arabs. He taught that, Arabia was a Moorish colony with Mecca as its capital. and, the entire Arab race, including Muhammad's, is mixed with Moorish blood. The gathering lasted for an hour; he wished he had more time. Usually, after Dwayne Bey opened the meeting and gave his portion, other brothers would go to the podium and give their portion. it was a lot of knowledge, and James enjoyed learning. Since the meetings were short, he'd use the time he had in his cell to study his Circle seven and his legal work.

That weekend, James sat in the visiting room talking to Zaria about her move to college.

"I'm not surprised."

"Why'd you say that?"

"Because when I talk to you, it seems as if your distant like your holding something to your chest."

"I didn't know how to tell you."

"All you had to say was, James I'm going to Atlanta to attend Spellman isn't hard to say."

"I didn't know how'd you'd react. I thought you'd be mad because I told you I was going to the U of M."

"Hey, what can I say. I sit in chains all day listenin to a bunch of nigga's lie and act like idiots."

"Well, I just want you to know, I'll stay in contact, and come visit during spring break."

James leaned back in his seat and felt as if she was abandoning him."O.k. that's cool, I'll see you when you get time off and stay in contact through the mail."

Zaria sat looking at James wondering why he was so blunt and distant. He didn't smile or joke anymore, it was as if he was a different James that she knew. They sat drinking soda, and talking for an hour, until it was time for her to leave. James got up, gave Zaria a hug and a kiss on the cheek, and went back to the madness of C-House.

James had been in the unit for about an hour, when he saw the folks and natives get into it. He was already aware of the rules- all blacks fought together in any racial situation. His first punch was thrown at a native dude fightin' with one of the folks, named O.J.. James hit him from the side, and he hit immediately smashed into the floor from the force of the blow. As he and 0.J. were letting their feet do the rest of the talkin; O.J., was hit with a lock in a sock from behind.

James immediately tackled the guy, so he couldn't get another swing. As he was on the floor trying to wrestle the lock in a sock away from the guy, O.J. had gathered his senses, and quieted the native guy with a punt to the head.

James grabbed the lock in a sock, turned, looked at the crowd of guys fightin, zeroed in on a native guy fightin Bugg, and rushed in that direction with the lock in a sock raised above his head, with one swift blow to the guys head James saw him grab his head and scream. As he ran from the blow, James could see the blood spurting from his face- it excited to the point, that he chased him down the flag screaming and hitting him in the head until the guy crumbled to the floor.

James stood over him, hitting him with solid blows to the head as he lay unconscious. James pulled back to land another blow to his head, when he was rushed into the cell bars by a native guy. His head hit the cell bars, and he could feel his grip loosen on the sock. As he was gathering his senses, he felt punches to his head and face. A few seconds later, J-Stone and G Mac rushed the guy with a fury of blows and kicks, that made him forget that his interfering with James beating his cousin to death wasn't an option.

James stood up and looked around the unit for another person to wrap the lock around their head. It had been at least five minutes into the fight, when the squad came in with a German Shepard and mace for everyone that was on the flag. James got in a few more swings, then he felt the mace, and all he could do was find a spot, where he couldn't get hit without him being able to protect himself. Then he felt someone grabbing him, throwing him to the floor, and handcuffing him. He laid there, mace burning his eyes and face thinking, what the fuck is this. James was snatched up off the floor, forcefully escorted to the segregation unit, placed in the shower, stripped naked, and placed in a cell. Though he was put in the shower to wash the mace off, he ran water over his face to stop the burning. Later, he sat there on the edge of his bunk touching the side of his face where he was hit, and looking at his knuckles, that were slightly swollen from hitting not only other people's heads, but the floor from a few miscalculated swings.

James, made his bunk, laid back on his pillow, and listened to everyone yell and forth about what happened, and how they beat people down; and how they couldn't wait to get out of the hole to repay a few punches that were received. James could care less, whenever he was released from seg, he would let his hands or lock in a sock speak for him. As he sighed and decided to go to sleep, he heard Wayne Mo call him. Damn, he thought.

"What up bruh?"

"Listen here Charlie, boy that shit was like Pontiac bruh."

"Like who?"

"Pontiac.

"That's one of the joints in Illinois."

"Oh. O.k."

"Yeah, Charlie. We about that business. Lil' bruh, I saw you in action. I had my fat ass on the front line too Charlie."

James laughed. "Yeah, I'm sure you did what you had to do."

"I know one thang, that damn mace ain't no hoe. That shit got all in my nose and ears them craka's ain't shit. They don't like to see us come together like that, that's why they come in with all that hoe shit they be on. If it was us gettin the beat down, we'd still be in the unit."

"Yeah bruh, they hate us with a passion." J-Smooth interrupted.

"Yeah, but they hoes love us tho."

"I hear ya pimpin. Them funky pink toes do love some black dick, don't they?"

"Ow, ow, ow, ow; they sure do Mo," said J-Smooth."

"James you ever had a pink toe bruh?"

James thought about Lisa. "Yeah, you can say that."

"Hol up. You can say that. What does that mean?"

"Yeah bruh."

"Where she from?"

"Fargo, she moved to Minneapolis a few years back."

"Ow, ow, ow, ow. You gotchu a piece of Paul Bunyan pussy, huh?"

James laughed. "I guess so, if that's what you wanna call it."

"Boy, you's a cold piece. I ain't never had a hoe from Fargo. Listen, I done pimped some exotic hoe's, but ain't never entered Paul Bunyan's territory."

"Listen Charlie. James is a true playa. He was just up there with a girl from India; I'm tellin you, I saw the pictures. Charlie, he be tryin to play possum on us J-Smooth."

J-Smooth responded. "Hey, they say the game is to be sold not told. Ow, ow, ow, ow. It's a cold thang ain't it?"

James sat there listening to J-Smooth and Wayne Mo talk about all the hoes they had, seen, and wanted. Their conversation carried James until he fell asleep. He had been in seg for two days listening to people talk about the time they had received from the riot. James heard 120, 180, 200, and thought that was a far cry from the 30 days he'd just done. He didn't know what was going to happen, so he waited to see what fate brought him.

James paced in his cell, thinking about the legal work he had read, when two guards showed up at his cell to take him to the discipline officer. He sat in a metal framed chair with a plastic seat reading the report. The hearing officer reminded him, they had him on camera fighting at least two people, and he used a weapon, so the offer was 200 days in seg, or he could go to a hearing and get the max of 360 days or more. James thought about it, and signed for the 200 days. He figured, what's the point. He'd sit back in seg and study the law.

CHAPTER SIXTEEN

200 DAYS

J ames was escorted back to his cell. As soon as he sat on his bunk, he heard Wayne Mo. "Hey Charlie, what they say?"

"I signed for 200."

"What, them damn cracka's ain't shit. Why'd they give you all that time?"

"They say I used a weapon, and fought more than one person."

"Fuck that shit, so mothafuckin what. They meant to say, since you didn't fuck no nigga's up, we gone throw the book atcha."

"I guess bruh. I ain't trippin. I'm in prison either way. Hey, let me kick back. I got some legal stuff to read."

James really needed time to pace and continue the mock argument with the justices from the United States Supreme Court. He was shocked when he heard the count bell ring. He had been talking to himself for the last six hours, if not more. He thought, he had to stop doing that or he'd keep losing track of time. And, the time he needed to study his legal work was important.

Two hours later, he was pacing into the evening. The segregation schedule wasn't bad. They came out for an hour each day, and half hour on the weekends. The situation that got James back there, led the segregation lieutenant to keeping the blacks separate from the natives. James didn't mind, it wasn't as if he was scared to introduce his left and right to someone if they cared to say hi. You can't tip toe in big foot country was James' motto. And, he would stand on that until his head hit the pillow in his casket.

They let James out with eight other guys. He had an hour to use the phone, work

out and take a shower, he skipped the phone, and spent forty minutes on the weights. He worked out, hit the shower, and went in and started pacing.

James' thought was interrupted by Officer Palmer. Palmer was a regular officer in the segregation unit. He was a pot bellied pudgy guy with short cropped black hair, and he wore a wedding ring that seemed as if it were going to cut his finger off, if his fingers got any fatter. James thought he was cool, he came to work, did his eight hours, and left. "Hey, you o.k.?"

James was in deep thought, looked up, and said; "Huh."

"You o.k., I see you pacing and talking to yourself again."

James stared at Palmer, thinking he had been pacing again and lost track of time while he was pacing. "I'm ok. I just have a lot on my mind, that's all Palmer."

"Well, if you need anyone to talk to, let me know. Pointing at the tray of food sittin in the food slot.

"Are you going to eat this?" James hadn't noticed they served lunch.

"Nah, I'm cool."

"I'll leave it here in case you get hungry. I leave at 2:20 I'll get it before I clock out."

"Thanks man." Palmer walked off thinking, I've seen that a thousand times. They come in with hopes and dreams, and leave with nightmares and psyche meds. I'll talk to Jan and have her come talk to him. James' doing his usual.

A few days later, James was doing his usual pacing when a skinny white woman with a long dark brown pony tail, wearing round framed glasses, holding a file close to her flat chest.

"Hello Mr. Blakely, I'm Dr. Thompson, how are you doing today?"

"I'm cool, what's up with you?"

"I work for the psychology department. I usually come see guys their first 90 days of their segregation sentence; but I was given a call to come see you. You seem to be pacing, and talking to yourself."

James stared at her for a second and took in how she dressed in dark brown jeans, and an off-white blouse, looking nerdy. Though James' thought about her looking like a nerd was correct, he would see how sinister she really was. " I'm cool. I just have a lot on my plate."

"It's alright to have a lot on your plate. It's when you start missing meals , and aren't cognizant when people approach you is where the problem lies. Are you in contact with your family?"

"Yeah, I talk to them all the time, and they come to see me on the weekends."

"What do you do to keep busy?"

"I read case law and study Moorish Science.'

"What do you talk to yourself about?"

"I recite a lot of case law I read."

Looking at her notes at how much time James had. She thought, this is easier than I thought, she'd have to call Mr. H and let him know not to worry. As long as James sat in the segregation unit, she was sure she could work something out for Mr. W, lord knows she needed a miracle to satisfy his need to keep James in prison. "How are you sleeping?"

"I sleep good."

"What does good mean?"

"I don't know, I go to sleep when I get sleepy."

Dr. Thompson wrote down in her note pad, seems to be losing track of time. "When

You're in population, do you pace in your cell?"

"I guess, I pace so I can think, not because I have a problem."

"No, no, I didn't say you had a problem. I just want to gauge how much sleep your getting."

"I guess I'm gettin the regular amount."

"On a scale of 1 through 10, how anxious are you throughout the day?"

"Uh, I'd say, maybe a six." Dr. Thompson nodded and wrote down Xanax. How about, I prescribe you an anti-anxiety medication to control the pacing, and it'll help you relax so you can get some sleep."

"Nah, I'm cool on the pills."

"O.k., what I'll do is come check on you periodically; would that be ok.?"

"If you want to."

"O.k. Mr. Blakely, you have a nice day." As she walked away she thought, this may be harder than I thought, I'll have to see what Goldstein thought about this. She had to get that monkey off of her back, so she could get her life back in order.

CHAPTER SEVENTEEN

THE OTHER SIDE OF THE GAME

James and Gomez had gotten close since Gomez was teaching and showing James how the law operated. They would sit and talk through the vent in the back of the cell after breakfast until 10 O'clock count. James had no idea Gomez knew all the stuff he taught him. He not only taught him the law, he taught him how to read people's personality traits. The thing that made James respect Gomez was when he let him read his paper work. James hadn't asked to read it.

He assumed Gomez was a sex offender and he left it at that. One night Gomez knocked on the slab of metal between the cells and handed James a large brown envelope with Gomez's name on the cover. James sat on his bed opened it and read a letter Gomez placed on top of the information. "Little brother. I know you heard about the rumors about me. I'm only showing you this because you're the only person who deals with me no matter what people say, including your brother's. It takes courage to follow your own spirit. Read this, and I'll get it back in the morning."

James looked at the first sheet of Gomez's indictment. It read. Four counts of first-degree murder. James sat in astonishment when he read the other four counts of kidnapping and attempted first-degree murder. Damn, he thought as he read the rest of the indictment. He read that Gomez was robber of four kilos of cocaine in St. Paul by four people. Gomez tracked down the people who had robbed him of the four kilos, got in their house, hog-tied everyone tied plastic bags over their heads and slit their throats.

While he was leaving a fifth person who happened to be in the house was coming down the stairs while Gomez was coming up the same stairs to check and see if the house was empty. Sheila Martinez saw Gomez, ran back up the stairs and into the bedroom. Gomez gave chase. He thought he had her trapped in the bedroom. When he reached out to grab her, she broke away from him and jumped through the bedroom window.

Gomez ran back down the stairs to catch her. When he headed to the back of the house looking for her body, he saw she had survived the fall form the second story of the house. He headed to the alley, and saw her hiding in between the garage and a tall wooden fence. When she saw Gomez she started screaming to avoid attracting attention from nosy neighbors, Gomez shot her four times and disappeared into the night; his only mistake was not making sure she was dead.

Three months after she healed from her wounds, she told St. Paul homicide detectives how she sat with her brother and four of his friends and laid out a plan to rob Gomez of four kilos of cocaine. She told them the initial plan was to rob and kill Gomez, but opted to rob him because they thought he didn't know where they lived. She was the only one who didn't pay with her life. Eight months later Sheila Martinez testified in Gomez's trial. Now, James sat in a cell reading his paperwork, thinking , damn, I would love to get out and pay Sheila Martinez a visit.

The next morning, James gave Gomez his paperwork back and let him know he had his back whenever he needed anything. After Gomez finished his set of pull ups." Yeah little brother, it's a mess sometimes. Just when you get shit in order, its' always someone lurking in the shadows to take you down."

"I hear you," said James sand began doing his set of pull-ups. Stretching his arms. "At the same time, it's the price we pay for livin a hard knock life."

"I don't think it matters what your life style. I think its just people who enjoy being jealous and envious, look where we are. These dudes put jackets on people without knowing the facts."

Smiling. "Believe me. It's a tight as jacket too."

"It's strange. The rats get all the love while the real ones get the shaft. Like ol' girl, that bitch was bogus from jump. When it's time to pay the piper, a mothafucka always gotta do some coward shit."

"I'm 50 years old. I've seen a few things in my short life and I'll tell you this; there's nothing new under the sun. Gomez started walking backwards while he was talking to James, accidently bumping into a member of the Aryan brotherhood. "Excuse me bro" said Gomez.

"I ain't your fuckin bro fuckin chomo." James didn't let him get another word out. He took three quick steps and punched the slender white guy in the nose, as he bent at the waist trying to figure out where the punch came from. James cupped the back of his head with both hands and an his knee into the guys forehead. James' actions took the other Aryans by surprise.

Their reaction was slow. Gomez was the slow reaction and rushed the other two Aryans with solid blows to their faces. Though he was fighting two guys he wasn't doin too bad, with the exception of catching a few punches to the head himself. As the Aryan James was fighting laid on the ground in his blood, James rushed to help Gomez. James came up behind a short fat guy and gave him a blow to the back of his head that made him yelp.

"Shit bro." and grab his head. By the time he figured out someone was behind him, James followed the punch up with a punch to his ear and ended his reign of terror on the Aryan with a choke-hold. James held him until he slowly slumped to the floor. As he backed up to help Gomez stomp the guy he was fighting. He was tackled.

All he heard was the guards yelling, "get down, get down." He and Gomez were restrained, cuffed and placed in isolation cells naked. James sat naked on the concrete slab they called a bed with no remorse for what he had done. He wished he could've gotten more time to let the Aryans know how much he loved stompin on the swastika's tattooed on their necks. James sat thinking, racist ass bitches wait til i get out this cell.

Three hours later, he was given a mattress, a blanket with no sheets or a pillowcase. He yelled to the guards. "I'll bet if I was one of them white boys ya'll give me a big fluffy mattress, pillows, and a quilt made by my grandma."

A guard responded, "You definitely don't want to be anyone of them. They're in infirmary trying to figure out what's not broken." James laid the blanket on the plastic mattress and laid-back feelin good about what he'd done.

After being in the isolation cell for two days James was escorted to a cell on the bottom galley with a plexi glass covering the cell bars and metal mesh. Pointing at the cell. " What's this?"

"The lieutenant wants you down here because this is your second violent incident," responded the guard.

"Are you serious?" shrugging his shoulders.

"Hey. I just do what he tells me."

Shaking his head in disbelief." This is bullshit."

James went in the cell and noticed his property was there. Once he thought about his legal work his isolation didn't matter. He made his bed and placed all of his items in order, grabbed his legal cases and read.

An hour later, James was pacing the floor.

The next day, Since James was given an additional 90 days for the fight he was placed on max custody status so he couldn't come out of his cell and exercise with more than one person. That was cool with him; he had more space to himself. And he didn't have to worry about anyone gettin their head beat in overdoing something stupid.

James was let out of his cell for his one hour of exercise. He walked down the flag to the exercise section, as he turned the corner to go to the weight machine he saw Gomez working out. "Ahh, shit. What up Gomez?"

"Hey little brother."

"How long you been back here?"

"About three minutes. My cell is around the corner."

"I was wonderin why that cell I walked past was open. Shit. We're two cells apart."

"I can still talk to you through the vent. They ain't stopped shit little brother."

"Phew old men you can throw them things."

"Ah, you know I'm old school I grew up fighting. I used to box as a youngster when I was in Texas."

"You ever go pro?"

"Nah, boxing is just the Texas culture. Texas is about beautiful cars, beautiful women, kilos, and boxing. You better believe it."

"How much more time did you get?"

"90."

" Yeah me too.

"What was up with them white boys?"

"I told you, when people put jackets on you it can get bad."

"How come you don't show people what you showed me?"

"Why, so people can be around me because I did what they won't do. These guys are petty criminals-I live the culture, they want to be a part of that, but they haven't passed the test. Most of these guys use drugs instead of sale then. If I give one of these guys a kilo they'd put it up their nose or in a pipe and pretend to be sellin drugs. My people live on both sides of the border little brother so i have access. I planned on openin shop in St. Paul, but this situation went down. The only thing that keeps me here is that witness. Other than that, I'd be movin that A-1 pericoooo."

"I definitively agree with you. I may not have been movin keys but I know I wouldn't be broke,"

"Now, we have to deal with these guys in here with the petty bullshit they stay on." Hunching his shoulders. "This is the other side of the game little brother." They skipped the workout and talked for their exercise. After they took showers and headed to their cells James sat in his cell reading he hadn't noticed that the plexiglass muffled the sound of other people's voices. Maybe the cell was a plus, he thought. He didn't mind being isolated as long as he had his clothes, legal materials, minus the bright light, he was cool. And he could hear Gomez whenever he called him. James found it hard to see the punishment aspect of the cell he was in.

Three days later his incessant pacing was interrupted by Dr. Thompson. "Hello. Mr. Blakely."

"Call me James."

"Uh. O.k. James. why James?"

"That's my name."

"I don't see any nickname or street name in your file. Do you have one?"

"No. My name is James. I'm not gimmick nor do I need another name."

"You seem irritated. Are you o.k.?"

"How would you be if you were in a cell?"

"I imagine! ---"

Interrupting her response. "That's the problem. You have to imagine this."

"I don't."

"So how are you getting along?"

"Why do you ask me the text book questions?" What do you mean?"

"Listen. I know you ask certain questions. Jot down the answers and cross-reference them with the answers in the DSM4 booklet. I just look like this."

"I see you know your stuff."

"I don't know everything. But, I know how you try to read my personality to see if you should place me in a situation I don't need to be in."

Raising her eyebrows. "Oh really?"

"Yeah. I'll tell you how you can help me." Thinking of telling her to suck his dick." Never mind. Listen. I have some reading to catch up on I'll talk to you later." She stood there watching James sit at the metal desk reading. She realized he wasn't going to talk and walked away.

When she walked away, James got up to see if she had gone. Cool. That bitch is the other side of the game too, he said to himself.

It had been about a month since James had heard from Amy. When he received the letter in the mail he figured it was about time. He opened the letter and found that the court of appeals had reversed his 40 year sentence on the second-degree murder to 20 years plus the good time he received while sitting in the county jail.

James had to do at least 19 year's for something he didn't do. There had to be a way out of this situation.

CHAPTER EIGHTEEN

BIG FOOT COUNTRY

The next day James showed Gomez the response to his appeal. Gomez congratulated him on the sentence reduction. James wasn't satisfied. Gomez reminded him of the time that he was doing and compared to what James was doing, Gomez would trade anytime.

"Damn bro. This might be cool that I don't have to serve a long sentence, but something's gotta shake."

"I hear ya James. You only have a few years left. You'll be young when you get out, kick back, get some college under your belt and go out there and make it happen."

"I can't let this go." Holding up the court's opinion. "They put me in here for something I didn't do. Somebody's gotta pay bro. There's gotta be a way. I guess it's like you said, it's a big ass cold blooded scheme. I wish I knew how they did it because I would surely make them pay for this shit."

"There is a way. But, you always have to remember, it's dangerous tip toeing in big foot country."

Looking at Gomez with his eye brows raised.

"Whatchu talkin about Gomez?"

"It starts with your name. Always remember your name is your property, that's how they keep us in here. They use your name as a vessel or straw man so they can make a dollar. When was the last time you spelled your name in all capital letters?" Looking at James' reaction to his comment. " Yeah, I see that look. Now the lights are on. That prison number is a CUSIP number, it allows the state to sell and trade the bond, the bond being your birth certificate."

Shaking his head in agreement. "What's a CUSIP number?"

"A111 bonds have a CUSIP number. It means committee on uniform securities identification process number. it's essentially a six digit tracking number for the certificate of stocks in the commodity and security exchange. You have brokerage firms like AG Edwards or Merrill Lynch who contract to sell all the prison bonds. Then the Paine and Webber Group provides securities for the prisons and sells the bonds. They act as the United States of America Corporation."

Rubbing his chin in deep thought. "Damn. That's deep."

Pointing at James. "No. That's big foot country lil' brother. These bonds are sold to China, Russia, Japan or any other country that chooses to buy them.

Pointing at himself. "We are a commodity. Once we hit that courtroom and the admiralty bond is filed in connection with the litigation, it's a wrap. Somehow 200 years ago when ol' Abe allegedly released the slaves, the writers of the Constitution slid that 13th Amendment slavery clause in there. Make no mistake about it, it's been planned."

"So. What about the attorneys?"

"Their sleep to the beat. The judges, prosecutors, and attorneys are members of the bar association. They are obligated to the bar. If they come to court arguing that your property has been seized without due process they'll be blacklisted and never work again. You'll see them working at McDonalds or something."

"So. This is a lone ranger project?"

"You got it. The penal system is a huge financial market for the United States. Once you enter the system that agency that is holding your social security number they call a bar code has a floating bond for 10 grand a day with your name on it. The bonds are bundled periodically and sold through bonding companies, turned into promissory notes and then bank securities." James sat listening to Gomez tell him how the scheme works. He knew that if he could expose this and get his freedom. 20 years was something he wasn't going to do. As he sat there thinking about how to get control of his straw man, the guard told him his hour was up. He shook Gomez's hand and returned to his cell.

Once he got in his cell he wrote down some of the things Gomez told him. he would start researching this through the state law library since he couldn't go to the prison law library to do the research, he would do it in his cell. With the information Gomez gave him and Gomez being a few cells down he'd be alright.

It took a few weeks for his legal request to get to him since the state law librarian delivered mail on a bi-weekly basis. James opened his mail and began reading. After a few hours of reading, he sat in amazement wondering how is it that this could happen. He sat and thought about the United States being a republic known as the United States of America, or the Continental United States. And the Constitution is supposed to be based on common law, but 100 years ago lawyers in league with the international bankers realized that a separate nation existed by the same name.

Congress created Article I Section II, Clause 17. And, the United States is in fact known as the Federal United States. And has exclusive control over anyone who is a citizen by way of the 14th amendment. That meant James was tangled up in the bullshit just because he was born in this mothafuckin country.

James sat up all night studying how the system was set up. He thought it was important to understand the origins and development of the system before he went into attack mode. As he studied he found that in 1938 the nation went bankrupt and was owned by its creditors, the International bankers. As a result of the bankruptcy, Congress and President Roosevelt mortgaged the national debt. The people had gone from being sovereigns over the government to subjects under the government with the stroke of a pen. It was through the use of selling birth certificates to discharge he debt with limited liability, instead of paying the debt with gold or silver coin.

To complicate and further dupe people, they changed the way the system of law operates. It went from public law to private commercial law, with the help of the United States Supreme Court, they blended the procedures of law with procedures of equity, which renders all U.S. Supreme Court decisions based on public policy instead of public law. These are some crafty moth-afucka's, thought James.

As he thought about what was goin on, he found himself pacing and muttering. "My name is my property." His muttering was interrupted by Gomez calling his name.

James responded. "What up?"

"You alright down there little brother?"

"I'm cool."

"I've been calling you for an hour. I thought you were sleep."

"Nah. I was studying this conspiracy."

"Yeah little brother, it's a mess ain't it?"

"Man you mean to tell me we steal, kill, rob, and wok for money that's not even there."

"Yeah. Those are the federal reserve notes young man."

Shaking his head in disbelief. "How the fuck does someone give me an 1.0.0. And act like it's real money?"

"We're being ruled a by a de facto government, under color of law that's used to control us. That's why they need the straw man. without it they can't extract the finances from us. See. in order for it to work, the corporate states have to accept the benefits offered by the federal government.

Then they're obligated to obey the Congress of the federal United States and assume their portion of the equitable debts to the international banking houses for the credit loaned. The credit is then given to the states in the form of federal grants and predicated upon equitable paper. It's a cold game, ain't it?

"Yeah. Sure is:

James sat and studied the monetary system his entire time in seg. Once he was released, they put him in C-house and Gomez went to A-house. James got a job at the license plate factory and the studies the system in his spare It was hard to run this across the other guys. They were too caught up in being a pimp, a major cocaine boy or a rapper. James thought, this is like night of the living dead; these goofy ass nigga's Shit. These other cats too.

They're all being duped and don't even know it.

James almost had to beat this cat up named Lahtee. James figured since he was a five percenter he knew better. Lahtee told James something about Clarence 13x and that he's a god and some more shit James wasn't tryin to hear.

As James walked away Lahtee told James he was unconscious. James spun on his heels and asked him if he knew his name was his property. Of course he didn't have a clue so he made a sad attempt at trying to insult James by calling him a conspiracy theorist. As James eased close to Lahtee to punch him in the mouth Wayne Mo came out of nowhere and grabbed James. " Let's walk Chalie Walie."

James looked at Wayne Mo. "Good lookin out Mo. I was finna knock his teeth out."

"Come on bruh, that nigga don't do shit but smoke crack and come to prison every year. You gotta ignore him and keep your thoughts to yourself."

Shaking his head in agreement. " Yeah you right Mo. Fuck that stud."

The next few days James spent his time reading the literature he received from the law library. he saw Gomez in the law library several times a week. That kept him in tune with a lot of the things that weren't written down in books. James sat in his cell on the weekends talking to himself and studying the law: The more he studied the more he was obsessed with how the monetary system worked. He found the system of negotiable paper bonds all corporate entities of government together in a vast network of commercial agreements and altered the judicial system from one under common law to a legislative Article I court or tribunal system of commercial law.

And the people brought before the courts are held to the letter of every statute of government on all levels unless they have exercised the remedy provided for then within that system of commercial law. So if James could prove he was forced to accept a so-called benefit offered, or available him from the government. He could reserve his former right under common law and not be bound by any contract, or commercial agreement, that he did not enter into knowingly, voluntarily, or intentionally.

Since all contracts signed by Roosevelt are not genuine contracts, James had to get hold of his straw man and obtain his release.

The first thing James learned from Gomez was to get a UCC I financing statement from the Secretary of State Office, fill it out, and send it back with a security agreement so he'll have proof that his straw man is copywritten, then he could discharge debt and be a free man.

That week James did the usual prison routine. It had been almost two years since he had been incarcerated and a lot, went down. Joe had gotten into a shootout with the police and lost that battle. Zaria moved to Atlanta to attend Spellman College. He got letters from time-to-time. Lisa seemed distant. he figured big dick bob was payin her a visit. He didn't think about it too much because he'd be out there soon enough and he'd start all over.

He learned a lot from Gomez. Since he knew how the game worked, who could stop him. And of course he had to make sure he paid a special visit to Mr. Lenways family. He never forgot how to serve revenge.

One afternoon James and Wayne Mo were walking to the dining hall when officer Nelson approached him about not having his i.d. on.

James took his i.d. from his shirt pocket and clipped it on his shirt pocket. Nelson then told James to give him his I.D.

James ignored him and kept walking because he knew Nelsons racist ass always fucked with Brotha's about some punk shit so he'd take the write up instead of giving him the joy of playin fuck boy games. Nelson said in a loud voice, "Hey, you, stop and give me your damn I.D." James continued walking to the line to get his meal. Nelson approached him and snatched James' I.D. from his shirt.

Before Nelson could get a word out, James hit him with a right punch that knocked his I.D. out of Nelsons hand, and sent nelson sprawling into a crowd of on-lookers. James stood there with his fists tightly balled and screamed, "bitch, "at the top of his lungs, jumped on top of Nelson, and began pounding his fists into his face. Wayne Mo stood there in disbelief watching the blood gush from Nelsons' face, it was so much blood, it was hard to tell where it was coming from. Nelson must've tried to grab James after he hit him, because he lay there with both his hands clutched slightly out stretched in front of him, that didn't matter. James straddled him and landed the hardest punches he could throw at Nelsons face. Once the squad arrived, it was over.

A few minutes later James was standing naked in a cell scream-in, " I'm sick of this shit; the system has stolen my property and now you wanna fuck with me." James lost control to the point where he went from banging his fists on the glass fronted door to banging his head on the door until it began to bleed. James screamed, " fuck you, my name is my property. Fuck you."

The segregation lieutenant made the decision to use the ex-traction team to strap James down to a restraint board, so he wouldn't hurt himself by banging his head on the walls and door. It took the extraction team a few minutes to get James out of the cell and onto the board. Once they strapped his legs and wrists down, he wouldn't stop screaming and trying to get loose. It got to the point where they called Dr. Goldstein, the overnight psy-chiatrist. Dr. Goldstein made his way to the segregation unit and evaluated James' condition, he felt that James was out of control and rambling about the system, his name, and the Conspiracy. He had to be delusional and a schizophrenic with a trait of post Traumatic stress syndrome.

Dr. Goldstein has saw this same condition in Vietnam vets. He opted to inject James with heavy sedative that would calm him down. Dr. Goldstein approached James while he was strapped down. leaning over James. " Hello Mr. Blakely, my name is Dr. Goldstein, I'm going to give you a shot that will make you feel a little better and calm you down."

"Fuck you, let me outta this shit; I haven't done anything wrong.". Screamed James.

"O.k., Mr. Blakely, here we go Dr, Goldstein said as he pierced James in the butt with the sedative."

James felt the prick of the needle and started screaming even louder; that screamed lasted for about 20 seconds before James felt the warmth of the sedative take over his body, he felt limp and clam, and slumped into an abyss of various thoughts.

CHAPTER NINETEEN

DR. FEEL GOOD

The next morning Dr. Thompson sat and read the incident reports along with Dr. Goldstein's report and recommendation. She decided that James should be transferred to the mental health unit at Oak Park Heights; they had the unit and doctors to deal with schizophrenia and severe delusional episodes.

She signed the transfer papers and hoped James would get better. James laid on the restraining board for half-hour, then the officers removed him; placed him in the isolation cell, and left him in the cell with a blanket and yellow suicide gown. James sat in the isolation cell thinking about how he couldn't wait to kill Nelson. He didn't care how much segregation they gave him, his next mission was murder. He had been in the isolation cell for three days when they came to transfer him. He thought it was amusing that it took six guards in full riot gear, with a camera to record them strip searching him, placing waist chains and shackles on him, to top it off, they placed a spit mask over his head, a dark blue helmet on his head.

Yeah this is real funny, thought James. As they lead him out the cell, he saw Dr. Thompson. In a cool mellow tone James said, "yeah, I see you over there doc. You see they got me strapped in like a serial killer, call me leather face. It don't matter, when I get out, I'll be at your doorstep. You think this is a joke. I have the keys to how the system operates and I will surely unlock the locks.

Dr. Thompson smiled at James and told James they'd take good care of him at Oak Park Heights, and they have an excellent mental health program for him there. James responded. "Does it look like I have any mental health issues? I know what you're up to. You think I'm stupid. Wait til I expose you too. I know you're up to something, my pops told me about you devils long time ago, and I know there are no strange happenings-It's all interconnected.

"Have a nice day Mr. Blakely; they'll take good care of you at Oak Park. She turned and waived at the guards in the security bubble so they could open the sliding door so she could return to her office. Dr. Thompson sat back in the leather reclining chair , sighed , and jotted down a few notes in James' psych file letting other doctors know that he was prescribed a dose of thorozine twice a day through injections to calm the conspiracy theories, delusions, and Schizophrenic episodes.

She opened her desk drawer pulled out a rubber stamp and stamped on his psych file MANDATORY INJECTIONS. She grabbed her purse, pulled out her cell phone so she could make the call. She sat nervously waiting for the other end to pick up. A deep scratchy baritone voice answered "yeah."

"Hey Mr. W this is Diane."

"O.K.."

"Uum, I finished my part of the bargain, are you going to hold up your end?"

"Certainly."

"They just transferred him to Oak Park and I made sure the injections were Mandatory, uh twice a day."

"Alright, then we're squared away." After she hung up, she swore she would never help Bob out again; if he drinks and kills someone else's kid she knew a divorce was the next best thing. In fact, that will be the best thing, she thought. She knew if James ever figured out what happened the blow back would be too much too handle, she definitely didn't want Melissa to be collateral damage in some judges power play.

Judge Weinberg sat back in his black leather chair and called Dr. Weinstein to cash in on a favor he owed him from college. He had to clean this up before his little donations were exposed. After this, he'd side step some favors and play it cool for a few years. He looked at his docket to see what the next case was, grabbed his robe and went to tend to justice.

The ride to Oak Park seemed long, may be it was because James was wrapped up like a mummy. He had patients; all he thought about was filing his UCC 1 financing statement and his security agreement, then this would be a thing of the past. He would make sure the future was bleak for a lot of people.

He arrived at Oak Park and was escorted down a narrow hallway to an intake section.

They decided to take him directly to the mental health unit and process him later. As James was escorted in waist chains, shackles, a helmet with a spit mask over his face he took note of the black and white tile in the corridor, it reminded him of a kitchen floor with extra wax. He was placed in an empty cell, with only a suicide gown and one blanket.

All he could think of was the bullshit these people were pulling. They removed the remnants of slavery from then told James to strip. He started to remove his orange jumpsuit, then he made his move.

The first punch landed on the nose of the guard closest to him. It was so sudden that the other four guards stood in shock, by the time they reacted James met the second guard with a fury of blows.

"Oh shit, grab him!" One guard yelled. It was too late, James was in full action, the sedative had worn off - all he could do was throw punches and scream at the top of his lungs. It took them to retreat out of the cell and come back with full riot gear and a shield to get James out of the jump suit and have Dr. Weinstein give him his first of the two injections. James managed to put on the yellow suicide gown before he sat on the naked mattress in a slump thinking about crushing Dr. Weinstein's head in.

His thought shifted to how he was going to get his property back and get out of this madness. Before he went into a deeper state of sedation, he wondered if Amy could get him out of this. He knew if he could get to a phone and tell her about this shit, he would be in a better place. Hmm, Amy and Moony will turn this fuckin place upside down, thought James.

His thought shifted back to the surroundings of the cell, looking around all he saw was staleness and thought, every time they come in here to shoot me with that shit, I'm fighting.

Three days later, Dr. Weinstein sat on the phone with Mr. W discussing what he should do with James' mail from the secretary of state that contained a UCC 1 financing statement and addendum. "Did he do a security agreement?"

"I didn't see one in his property."

"Well, shred it and I mean literally, shred it. Any mail that comes from that office contact me."

"O.k. sir." After Dr. Weinstein hung up the phone he immediately shredded the letter and forms. He surely didn't have time for Mr. W to expose his hidden absurdities- he hated this, he always locked the dorm room door when he was being his alter ego, Susan.

He thought that was a thing of the past until Mr. W called. He sighed as he listened to the shredder spit out the letter into the recycle bin. Before he wrote down a few notes in James' file, he thought Mr.W was always a sneaky bastard.

"Hey, how are things at the D.O.C. Dave?" "They're doing the usual. What can I do for you Mr. W?"

"I have an issue with your prisoners sending sovereignty crap to my office. I need you to fix it, and I mean like yesterday."

Running his hands through his salt and pepper grey hair, Dave Esty said, "I'll take care of it." After he hung up, he called the assistant commissioner, and told him to draft up a memo regarding UCC 1 filings- he made it clear that he wanted it to end ASAP.

James had been in Oak Park a week and he hadn't let up. He kept his promise to fight every time they came to put that shit in him. He paced back and forth thinking about UCC 1-207, as long as 12 could use that in conjunction with his signature he wouldn't be bound to a statute, commercial obligation, or any Commercial agreement he didn't enter into voluntarily.

Once he got his financing statement, he'd be in a better position to protect his property; and that cracked ass liberty bell would surely ring. He'd love to see hang em hig's face when he got that writ of error, puttin that mark on notice would be challenging that they had no jurisdiction to charge, convict, or sentence him.

He smiled when he thought about how allocation works in conjunction with common law. As he paced, he heard something slide in his door. He grabbed it and read. All he could do was squint his eyes when he read the memo's heading. Bogus UCC activity. He read on and saw that the commissioner was rejecting all information related to filling UCC forms; they are now contraband, how could they do this?

Shit, thought James.

Fuck these devils are really on some bullshit. This is proof that this shit is real. No wonder why my paper work hasn't arrived. All James could do was sit back and stare into space wondering how he was going to work his way around this bullshit. He wondered what Gomez thought. he hadn't replied to his letters, all he could do was think about what Gomez told him when he started this shit; Never tip toe in big foot country.

That evening, Dr. Weinstein and his suited up goons approached James' cell with the same ol' stiff as Mr. Blakely, we need to give you your shot. James gave the reply. Motion for them to come into the cell.

"Come and give it to me."

THE END OF PART I

ABOUT THE AUTHOR

Pepi McKenzie was convicted of first-degree murder in 1992. He has used his hard-knock lessons acquired from jailhouse pimps, lawyers, prisoncrats, and members of street organizations to pen urban mystery thrillers that speak to the ineffectual judicial systems that harbor and coddle corrupt judges, prosecutors, and crooked homicide detectives whose aim is to incarcerate those that live in American ghettos.

Pepi McKenzie's mission as a mystery writer is to bring urban mystery to the forefront by introducing the urban voices that are silenced by other mystery writers.

You can follow him @:
PepitheAuthor.com
Amazon.com/Pepi McKenzie
Pep The Author@Facebook.com
PepiMcKenzie@Facebook.com
Allsquarempls.com

www.ingramcontent.com/pod-product-compliance
Lightning Source LLC
Chambersburg PA
CBHW070525100726
47907CB00004B/988